I0733359

# MAID FOR HIM

## STARLING BAY BOOK 2

### SIENNA CARR

Author's Note

~

***Maid for Him*** is a STANDALONE romance. It is the 2<sup>nd</sup> book in the ***Starling Bay*** series. While you do not need to have read the first book, ***Winter's Kiss***, it might enhance your reading experience if you do, because many of the characters in this series appear in different books.

Starling Bay Series:

Whirlwind Kisses
Winter's Kiss
Maid for Him
Love Letters
Escape to Starling Bay (Books 1-3)
From Faking to Forever
Winter's Vow
Guarded Hearts
Table for Two
A Bouquet of Charm
Christmas Hope

Newsletter sign up: http://www.siennacarr.com/newsletter

"Please, Shay. I need something quick and easy. Something I can start today," Jenna pleaded.

"I know. I heard you. I heard you last night, and the day you arrived, Jenna. But you don't have to follow me into work." Her friend looked at her and made a face. Jenna felt useless, worse, she was beginning to feel like a burden. Returning to Starling Bay had seemed like a good idea a few weeks ago when she'd been sitting in her cockroach-infested room in a shared apartment, eating ramen noodles.

She had decided that enough was enough. Between working at the supermarket, and working as a waitress in the evenings, she barely had much money left over, and what she did have, she saved.

Starling Bay seemed like heaven, and it offered a new lease of life, and that was enough for her to pack her bags and return after twelve years.

But now that she had been here a few weeks, the doubts started to creep in. It wasn't a city, and didn't offer the job opportunities in such abundance. It wasn't exactly small, either, and it had changed. She didn't remember it being so expensive.

Or maybe, she'd been so dirt poor all her life, that *everything* was expensive.

She was here now and she had no choice but to make things work. This was going to be her fresh start, dang it, and there was no going back. "I have no money," she insisted. "And I'm camping out on your sofa. I need to get back on my feet." Her friend had no idea what it was like to be so broke. Jenna had a couple of hundred dollars to her name, and she was going to budget very carefully until she got a job. A *couple* of jobs, she figured, if it came to that.

"Look," said Shay, pushing up her glasses. "It's Monday morning, I need to get back into work mode, check my emails—"

"Please," Jenna begged. She didn't have the time to sit around waiting while Shay 'eased into work mode'. "Please. Can't you take a quick look now and see if anything's come up over the weekend? I'll leave you in peace, I promise." And then she would hound Shay later when she returned home from work in the evening.

Shay huffed out a breath and peered closer at her screen. "I've got a couple of cleaning jobs." She frowned. "Maybe not."

"I'll take it."

"No. I don't think this one is any…" Her friend's voice tapered away, and she moved her mouse pointer around. Jenna wished she could stand over her friend's shoulder and see the screen for herself instead of trying to decipher Shay's facial expressions.

"Whatever it is, I'll take it." She wasn't fussy.

"Ah, here's another one." Shay smiled.

"What is it?"

"Cleaning a group of small offices, or," she peered closer at the screen.

"Or?" asked Jenna, in her mind she had already accepted the first job.

"They need someone to clean for a few hours every morning at the preschool," Shay told her.

"The preschool?" She imagined this would be small and easy enough to do. How much mess did tiny kids make? "What was the first job?" she asked suspiciously. It seemed that there was something Shay wasn't telling her.

"You won't want it."

"You haven't told me what it is yet."

"Trust me. You won't want it."

"Is it cleaning toilets? Because I'll do it." She would do whatever it took.

"It's…uh…" Shay settled back in her seat, and folded her arms. "It's cleaning some rich guy's mansion—"

"I'll do it. Sign me up already."

Shay opened her mouth, and her lips twisted but no words came out. She eyed Jenna with a level gaze.

"How bad can it be? I'll do it."

"It's the Knight mansion."

These four words had the power to paralyze her. She snorted. "You've got to be kidding me. That thing is still standing?"

"Of course it's still standing."

"And they still live there?" Of course they did. Why would they not? The Knights were as old as the dinosaurs. They'd been here from the start. Generations of Knights had lived in the huge sprawling mansion in Glassmere, the exclusive end of Starling Bay. It was away from the busy town center and the bay, with the back of the house overlooking the ocean.

For Jenna, it represented extreme humiliation and she seethed at the mention of it.

"They don't live here anymore, only Reed does. His parents bought a ranch in Montana."

"They did?" Jenna imagined horses running wild on acres of land. "Why would you buy a ranch in Montana?"

"Because they can. What does it matter to you?"

Jenna shrugged. The lives of the rich were a continent away from her own. She was living with Shay, for now, because she couldn't yet afford to rent a small apartment of her own. Meanwhile, the Knights had left an enormous, fit-for-a-king mansion in which their son now lived, while they left to go and live on a ranch in Montana. It wouldn't surprise her if they'd bought a thousand-acre ranch out there. The Knights super-sized everything.

"I told you that you wouldn't want this one."

Jenna swallowed. "I'll do it. I'll clean his house." Of all the men she could have run into, and all the places she would end up in, it would have to be this one. "I need it." She really did. Reed Knight or not.

"Is this wise?" Shay asked.

"I need the money, and I will do a good job wherever you put me, but if this is the only position that is available, I'll take it. I'll work at that place, for him." She couldn't even bring herself to say the names. "I hate that they think they're better than us, and I hate that he thinks he can treat the likes of us as if we're—"

"You're still mad at him, Jenna! I'm not sure this is going to work out."

"I'm over it," Jenna said quickly. "It was nothing. He won't even recognize me, not with this." She gently tugged at her hair.

"Would it really be such a problem if he did?"

"I can't stand the guy so—" She stared at Shay, then smiled. "It's not going to be a problem."

"I can't afford to give this to you if there are going to be problems, Jenna."

"I'll be as good as gold, I promise. When can I start?"

"I'll need to check with his PA," said Shay.

"He has a personal assistant?" Jenna scoffed. "I'll bet he has a chauffeur, and a cook, and a gardener, and—."

"He keeps it simple, from what I've heard. He only has his personal assistant, more like a butler, say, and someone to cook for him and a maid to clean."

"The luxury of having these people in your life," Jenna muttered. "He doesn't cook for himself *at all?*"

"The cook's probably been in the family for years, like the butler. He doesn't need to do it, so why should he?"

"It's still surprising that in this day and age, a grown man needs someone to cook for him."

"You really have it out for him, don't you? I'm not sure you working for him is a smart move, for you or for me. I'm not sure I can place you there, Jenna. It would look bad on the agency if you messed up. It would look bad on me."

"I'll be good. I promise." She rushed to reassure her friend. "I'm curious to know what he's like now."

"If you keep your mouth shut, you might get to find out. Did you know he's engaged to be married this summer?"

"Poor woman," Jenna muttered.

"He's not as bad as he used to be."

"Easy enough for you to say."

"I was there that night as well."

Jenna looked away. Reed Knight had helped her up when she'd fallen down on the track one day. One of the most popular boys at the school, he had been polite, and concerned, and she'd been smitten. And when she and her friends had received an invite to his party months later, she'd been beyond excited. But that day had ended in a humiliation that she had carried around with her for years. Nobody had been in her shoes. Yes, Shay had been there with her, but Shay hadn't been the one they had laughed at.

"Let me call his PA and arrange for an interview."

"Great, because I'd like to start as soon as possible."

# CHAPTER 2

The sound of the ringing phone thundered in his ears. Reed reached out to grab it, but knocked the sleek handset off his nightstand instead.

And then his cell phone started ringing, and the noise sliced through his ears like a blade. He winced because his head felt as if it had been axed into two.

"Mr. Pennington?"

"No, it's Reed Knight."

"Oh, I'm sorry to disturb you, Mr. Knight. It's Shay Donovan from the recruitment agency."

"Who?"

"Shay, from the recruitment agency."

What in the blazes were they calling him for? And where was Pennington?

"You were looking to hire a maid?"

"Talk to Pennington."

"Mr. Pennington mentioned that he was away on vacation and to contact you directly. He said it was urgent."

Reed groaned, remembering. Trust his entire household staff to abandon him at the same time. "Ugh," he sat up and steadied himself on the bed. The room was spinning. "Can it wait?" he thundered, then winced as his head started to throb.

"Mr. Pennington said he wanted someone to start as soon as possible, and I've found just the right person. She's ready to start as soon as possible."

Reed put a hand to his throat. Inside, it felt parched. He didn't need anyone this week, and he could cope just fine alone.

"Shall I send her over, before she gets assigned somewhere else? You did say you wanted someone quickly?"

"I said nothing of the sort," he growled, standing to his feet and sitting back down again. Did Pennington think he couldn't handle anything by himself? Maybe Olivia, his fiancée, had put him up to it. That princess couldn't cook or clean, or do much else, as he was beginning to find out. He slammed the phone down, and sat back on the bed, resting his back against the headboard.

Going out with his friends hadn't been a good idea. He needed to get a handle on these late nights, but he hadn't seen Dylan and Rourke for weeks, not since the New Year's Eve party which Olivia had insisted on throwing.

What a farce.

He wiped a hand across his brow, thinking about the mess he was in. Some days he wasn't so sure it was pre-wedding nerves. Olivia didn't seem to harbor anything of the sort, and she was certainly an expert when it came to spending his money.

He gulped down half a glass of water and downed two painkillers, then grabbed his cell phone and checked his business emails, all from the comfort of his bed. Work never stopped, no matter what. He also had a few important calls to make, and got started with those.

He paced around the room as he made his calls, and when the doorbell rang, he ignored it automatically.

It wasn't until the doorbell rang for the fourth or fifth time that he remembered Pennington wasn't here, and Cecile, his cook, had gone away to care for her sister who'd had an operation.

"One moment," he said to the person at the other end of the line, then, when the doorbell rang again, "I'll call you right back." Annoyed, Reed quickly pulled on a pair of jeans. "Shouldn't have let him go," he muttered to himself. Damn Pennington and his two-week bird-watching trip to Costa Rica.

He sauntered downstairs and opened the door to find a woman standing on his doorstep. A pair of green eyes stared back at him, but it was her blue-tipped hair that grabbed his attention. "Yes?" he asked, not happy with the interruption because he hated when people wasted his time.

She was obviously here to sell something, because he didn't know who she was, and he hardly ever had visitors.

"I've come for the interview. Shay sent me."

# CHAPTER 3

"*Who*?" Reed Knight looked annoyed. For a split second Jenna's gut tightened, and she wondered if he would remember her.

"Shay Donovan…from the agency." She waited to see if the mention of her friend's name might jog his memory, but it didn't seem to.

As for Reed, he hadn't changed much at all. He was older, and the boyishness of his youth had long gone, but those hard blue eyes were the same. And the hair was less blond, more dark.

"I'm Jen—." But his cell phone rang and he answered it, giving a barely hidden look of disgust at her hair before continuing with his phone call.

She had been about to ask him if it was okay for her to prop the bicycle Shay had leant her up against the wall, but he wasn't even looking at her anymore and seemed more engrossed in his phone conversation.

It sounded like business. She didn't know where to look, and he hadn't asked her to come in, so she stood in the doorway. Her gaze lowered to his chest because he hadn't even put a shirt on.

"We'll talk later. I have a situation I need to deal with first." A look of annoyance swept across his face, and he appraised her, as if he wasn't sure he could trust her to come into his house. She held her breath, wondering if he had figured out who she was, but there was no flicker of recognition on his face. Good. She preferred it that way.

"Why's your hair blue?"

She bit back on her teeth. Because she liked experimenting, and blue-tipped ends made her feel different. Made her stand out. Plus it got her more tips at the restaurant where she'd worked. "Why are you half-naked?" she threw back.

His eyebrow lifted in shock, as if this was news to him. He stared down at his chest as if he had only realized now. "You might as well come in." He opened the door wider, then seemed to hesitate. "I told whoever called me, your boss, or whatever, that I didn't need anyone. I didn't expect her to send someone. Why did she?"

She had been about to step inside, but now stopped. Something in the pit of her belly told her that this wasn't a good idea. She didn't want this job *that* much, and he didn't seem to really want anyone here right now.

"I don't know." She stepped back. This wasn't going to work out. Not with this guy. He had been a douchebag at school, and signs were that he hadn't changed at all now. "I don't … I don't think this is going to…"

He snorted. "Don't worry, sweetheart, I'm not going to make a move on you. You're not my type."

She snorted. "You're engaged, and even if you weren't, you're *definitely* not my type."

"Do you want the job or not?" he growled. "Pennington said it was urgent, but it's not. But since you're here you might as well make yourself useful."

Could she put up with him for a few hours a day? She didn't really have any better alternative right now. She stepped inside.

"The kitchen's straight down the hallway, at the end. I'll be there shortly. I guess I should put a shirt on in case you hyperventilate." He had the audacity to laugh at his own joke.

She stood seething with quiet rage, forcing herself not to say anything. But it still wasn't too late to walk away.

Nevertheless, she walked down the long hallway, passing so many doors on either side that she lost count. How many rooms did this place have?

Did he really live here alone? Or with his fiancée? This place was huge enough for them both to have their own quarters.

She walked into the large, light and airy kitchen which was almost four times as big as Shay's entire apartment.

The décor looked expensive and she was almost too scared to touch anything. Running her finger down the countertops, she could see that they were a little dusty. Everything in here needed a wipe, and she wondered who cooked for him. For *them?* She wondered where his fiancée was.

"So," he said, striding in wearing a red sweatshirt. "Sit down."

*Please.* She wanted to scream at him. *Please.* He had no manners, and obviously thought he was above her station.

"Please," he said, when she hesitated. "And you can take your coat off." He took a seat on one of the stools along the kitchen island.

She preferred not to take her coat off, so that she could bolt right out of here if she needed to, but she sat down across from him.

"Experience?" he asked, mustering a huge breath, making her feel as if this was a drain of his precious time.

"I can clean." *What other experience did he need?*

"Where have you worked before?"

It was an embarrassing question, and she was extremely thankful he hadn't remembered her at all, because her answers would indicate how little she had accomplished. She'd left

Starling Bay broke, and was now returning broke. There was nothing as humiliating as knowing that more than a decade later, her financial circumstances, and life, weren't any better. She hated herself for it.

"I worked in Chicago at one of the local supermarkets, and in the evenings I would waitress."

"Two jobs?"

"Some people have to have many jobs. Not everyone's born with–" She was about to say 'privilege' but forced herself to bite her tongue. She needed this job. "With the…" she tried to think of something to say.

"The?"

"The ability to get a great nine-to-five job that's going to pay the rent."

"And cleaning experience?"

She hadn't done that before, not as a maid. She swallowed. "I've cleaned as a waitress—wiped tables and cleared dirty dishes, swept floors and done any deep cleaning that the night cleaning crew didn't do."

"You were part of a team," he muttered. "You likely weren't the only one. What about people's homes?"

She didn't know what this had to do with anything, and she had to force herself not to shoot off a cocky reply. Cleaning was cleaning. As if *he* knew anything about it. She'd bet he'd never had to wash a dish in his life. "I've cleaned homes."

"Yours, I presume?"

Her lips tightened. "Yes." He'd caught her. Shay was going to kill her, because she'd made Shay's recruitment agency look unprofessional.

"And you can start now?"

"Yes."

"Then you might as well get started now," he said. "I'll have some breakfast."

She stared at him so hard her eyes almost bugged out of their sockets. "But I'm here for the cleaning position."

"And we've determined that you barely have any experience of doing that."

"It's cleaning, for goodness' sake," she cried out, her voice raised in exasperation. And then, remembering her place and position, "How hard can it be?" She forced a smile. It almost killed her to do it, but she reminded herself that it was necessary.

"Do you want the job or not?"

This was the second time he had asked her that question, and she couldn't tell if he was toying with her desperation at needing the job, or whether he really was a total douchebag who loved playing with people's emotions.

Her jaw clenched, and she was torn between storming out of there or staying, but she knew she didn't have much to her name right now. Telling him to go to hell wouldn't put much-needed money in her pocket.

"I can pay you now for making breakfast." His voice teased, and she hated that even more. This rich, privileged and extremely lucky man was flaunting his power and his standing. And just like that time when she had been sixteen, he made her feel insignificant.

"Shouldn't you go through the agency?" He might think he could buy his way through everything, but she didn't want Shay to lose out on her commission.

"I can do whatever I want."

His reply left her dumbfounded. Reed Knight was as selfish and arrogant as ever. "You are *so...*" Rage tunneled up inside her like a tornado wanting to let loose.

*Hold it back, hold it. Hold it.* If she kept her teeth clenched tightly like this any longer, she'd be grinding down her molars.

"I am so...what?" He pulled out a twenty-dollar bill and held it out to her. Her past humiliation and shame flooded back. He must have seen something in her reaction, because, for a moment, his face turned serious. A sliver of sobriety raced over his features and he withdrew the bill, then placed it on the table.

"I'm sorry. I don't know what came over me." He got up. "I'm starving and kind of hungover, so if you could make me a couple of eggs on toast, I'd appreciate it. Money's on the table if you do."

Her jaw would have landed on the kitchen floor, if it hadn't been attached to her face. She couldn't wait to tell Shay how wrong she had been to think Reed Knight might have mellowed with age.

His cell phone went off and he answered it, walking out of the kitchen and leaving her to look around, wondering what she had gotten herself involved in.

It was Olivia on the line again.

"Have you calmed down?" he asked.

"It depends, can you take some time out to go through the honeymoon brochures with me?"

He paused, and told himself to calm down. "It's hardly a construction project, Olivia. It shouldn't be too difficult. Nowhere exotic, no more than two weeks, and—"

"But it's our honeymoon!" she cried, in a burst of hysteria.

"And I've told you I can't take too much time away, not in the summer, and not for a month. We can go for a longer break somewhere exotic, later in the year."

"But it's our honeymoon," she whined. "It's supposed to be special."

"I can't argue with you this morning, Olivia. I need to focus," he said, and hung up. He wasn't asking her to make a huge compromise, he was asking her to understand. For an ex-beauty queen, she seemed to think she could lead the millionaire lifestyle. She hadn't been like this when he'd met her. He tried to think back to last year, and the sweet, confident and friendly woman he'd met at the plush Manhattan Hotel. Olivia attracted attention wherever they went. Sometimes people recognized her as the beauty queen who almost made it to Miss America and became runner-up. People were dazzled by her tall thin legs, her long, long neck, and almost skeletal frame. She didn't exercise, but she didn't eat much either, and while she didn't look too thin because she dressed to impress, she was all bones and hardness.

She was a stunner. And that was one of the first reasons he'd noticed her, but back then she had been warm and friendly. He'd been captivated. After a couple of weeks of getting to know her, he'd whisked her away to St Barts, and wined and dined her at the small Caribbean Island. He'd been so taken in by her beauty, by the way people reacted to her, that he hadn't had much time to see what the real person was like underneath.

And now he was living to regret his hastiness.

Fed up, after another argument last night, he'd gone to the Blue Velvet Bar with his friends again.

Olivia wanted exotic destinations for a honeymoon, and she wanted to go for a month, but he couldn't take that kind of time off. Not with so many business ventures going on. He'd recently won the contract to refurbish the old movie theater here. He had obligations and responsibilities. He could go for a few weeks, but not halfway around the world, and definitely not for a month. Not right now.

In hindsight, he had set up the wrong expectations. Taking her to St Barts might have led her to believe that he could give her that type of life all the time.

He could. He so easily he could. But *he* didn't want that type of life. He was a businessman, fueled by ambition and the intoxicating smell of success.

It was a petty thing, arguing over honeymoon destinations, but it was one petty thing in a whole heap of them. He should have known that getting engaged to an ex-beauty queen wasn't going to be a dream ticket to happy-ever-after, but he was in love, or rather, he *had* been back then, and he'd believed they could make it work.

Come to think of it, why had he been in a hurry to get a two-carat diamond on Olivia's finger? As time went on he found himself pondering the answer to that question more and more.

And if he had been in love, then where was he now?

He wasn't sure, or couldn't face the truth. He hadn't yet decided which of the two it was, and an evening with his friends had been the perfect antidote to his stresses. Last night he'd come this close to telling them that things weren't so great.

*This close.*

But his friends believed he was ready and looking forward to getting married, and he didn't want to open a can of worms. And lately, he found himself wondering if it might not be too late to call the whole thing off.

The smell of fried eggs wafting towards him was comforting, and it enticed him back into the kitchen.

The new maid had slipped on an apron.

"Eggs," he said lightly, his mood brightening at the sight of toast and eggs and the coffee which she had already put on. He was impressed. She had already switched on the coffee machine and figured it all out, even where the coffee pods where. Pennington had had to explain to the last maid how to work it.

Morning coffee was his staple, and for that reason, this woman had already won some points. Too bad he'd acted like a complete moron towards her.

"You've made my day," he told her, sitting down to eat as she handed him the cutlery. "This looks good."

She pressed her lips together, as if she was holding back from saying something. "Don't hold back," he told her, digging his knife and fork into his food.

"Where are the cleaning supplies?" she asked, ignoring his request.

"In the utility room. I'll show you around when I've eaten."

"I can find it if you tell me where it is." She moved towards the door.

"It's two doors down on the left."

"I'll get started."

"I'll show you around the house later. There are certain parts upstairs, my fiancée's rooms, that you're not to go into."

"Understood."

"And it's light cleaning. Dusting and vacuuming. This house is too big for one person. Pennington has a professional company come in from time to time to clean the curtains, and polish the windows and the ornaments, so you won't need to get your hands too dirty."

"I don't suppose you've ever gotten your hands—"

He stopped chewing, and stared at her. She was a fireball this one, and it amused him. Nobody had ever had the guts to say a word out of line to him before. Even Olivia had said all the right things, before he'd slipped the engagement ring on her finger. "Dirty? I think is the next word you were going to say."

She chewed her lower lip. He took that to be a sign of unease, one that he was accustomed to seeing often.

The maid said nothing.

"Don't forget your twenty dollars," he reminded her.

That had an effect; it earned him a cold, hard stare. Maybe he'd been a little too out of line this morning. He'd been angry with Olivia, but he'd upset the new hire. He put down his cutlery. "I'm sorry. That was a stupid thing to do."

She picked up the bill and slipped it into her pocket.

"These eggs aren't too bad."

"Hope you don't choke on them."

"That's not nice," he replied, suppressing a grin, because, for some reason, her comeback made him smile. He'd behaved like a jerk, but her feistiness told him she could take it.

"I'm supposed to clean your house, not be nice to you."

"That's right. You are the maid."

"I'm only putting up with your arrogance because I need the money," she answered back.

She was a testy little thing. He smiled as she walked away. This one was a spitfire. He liked that, and he wondered what Pennington would make of her.

# CHAPTER 4

*S*he needed a muzzle fit for a pit bull. At any rate, she needed to rein in her mouth. She'd been lucky that Reed Knight hadn't fired her on the spot.

The guy was a jackass, but if he could throw twenty-dollar bills around just because she'd made him breakfast, well, it was a better tip than she'd have received at the restaurant. He threw money around as if it was confetti, and she was more than happy to crawl around the floor picking it all up.

No. No more mouthing off and answering back like she had. She couldn't afford to get fired from this job. Shay would kill her

"He didn't recognize you at all?" Shay looked over the Roxy's Diner menu. Her eyebrows lifted in disbelief.

"No."

"I bet he did. I bet he did and he didn't let on, and you were too anxious to notice."

Jenna considered her friend's verdict, but ditched it. "Nope. He looked at my hair in disgust, but that was about it. There wasn't any flicker of recognition in his eyes." And when her friend seemed to find this hard to believe, Jenna added, "That man hasn't changed one bit. He's still as self-obsessed and selfish as ever."

"I'm surprised."

"I'm not," Jenna retorted. And to think she'd been worried about the past, that he might remember. Because it was something she'd never forgot.

"He's always been pretty civil when I've run into him," Shay continued.

"He's as vile as ever."

"I don't have that opinion of him."

Jenna turned and looked at her friend. "You were there that night, too. Surely you haven't forgiven him?"

"People change. I think he's changed, and I don't think he remembers that time," Shay remarked. "High school was a long time ago, Jenna, and you left Starling Bay before we graduated. It wasn't a big deal in the end."

"He turned us away, and they all laughed at us."

"We were teenagers!"

"How can you just forget about it?" Jenna couldn't. The humiliation of being turned away was bad enough, but falling down and ripping her skirt? She could still hear the collective laughter behind her, as she rushed away with her skirt in tatters and the side of her leg grazed.

"How can you not?" cried Shay. "You're the one who left Starling Bay. You didn't need to hold onto old grudges. And as he got older, he wasn't so bad."

"Wasn't so bad," mumbled Jenna under her breath. She wished Shay would have seen the way Reed Knight had behaved earlier today.

It didn't matter what Shay thought. Jenna knew she and the Knights were worlds apart. She'd had to leave Starling Bay because her dad had to move to where the work was. Uprooted from school at that age had been hard. Coming back to Starling

Bay had been harder than she had anticipated, especially with someone like Reed Knight rubbing her face in it.

"I still hate having anything to do with him," she declared. "The only reason I'm putting up with him now is because I need the money. I'd do anything, well, *almost* anything."

"You made him breakfast, that's a start," Shay reminded her. "But he shouldn't have asked you to do that. The job description distinctly specified cleaning duties."

"He's Reed Knight, remember," said Jenna in an I-told-you-so voice. "He can do whatever he wants. Anyway, here you go." She whipped the twenty dollar bill out of her purse and held it out for her friend to take.

Shay shook her head. "Dinner is my treat."

"It's a tiny contribution towards the rent."

"Jenna, no. Just pay me when you get paid."

"I did get paid…for making breakfast."

"I wonder where his cook was?"

"No idea. I didn't see her or his fiancée."

"He's got that huge place to himself," gasped Shay.

Jenna nodded. "I barely saw him. He stays in his study most of the time. I kept expecting his fiancée to appear. Come to think of it, I wonder why he never got her to make him breakfast."

Shay snorted. "You don't expect Olivia Sykes to cook, do you? I don't suppose she even knows where the kitchen is."

"When are they getting married?"

"Sometime in the summer."

"Summer?" asked Jenna. It was less than six months away.

"I'm surprised you didn't crack an egg on his head when he slipped you the money to make him breakfast."

"I was tempted to, but I needed the twenty dollars more than I needed my pride."

"Keep the money," Shay insisted. "Get settled and get yourself back on your feet first."

"At least let me go halves on the dinner."

"It's my treat," Shay insisted.

Jenna opened her mouth in protest. "First you get me the job, and then you take me out to—"

"Put that away," said Shay, interrupting. "I know how hard this is for you."

"Getting a job?"

"Being a maid to Reed Knight."

"Yeah." She sighed. How had she sunk so low?

"But it's only a stepping stone to better things, and you have the job. I mean, you made him breakfast. And he hired you on the spot."

"I don't think he had much choice after I turned up on his doorstep. He looked surprised to see me."

"You obviously made an impression."

"I think he was hungover and needed breakfast."

"Stop putting yourself down," Shay scolded. "Here's to a beautiful working partnership."

"You and me?" Jenna asked.

"You and Reed Knight."

Jenna made a face as if she'd smelled rotten eggs.

# CHAPTER 5

"I hope your sister gets better soon, and thanks for letting me know." Reed hung up. Cecile wasn't going to be back for another couple of weeks at least, and Olivia was holed up in her condo—or rather *his* condo. It was one of many he owned in Forest Heights, a new luxury development roughly ten miles away.

She had moved in with him after the engagement, but it wasn't long before she started inviting her friends over to stay the weekend. He was used to having his home to himself, and he was happy to have Olivia to share it with, but not groups of her friends. Every couple of weekends they would come over from Manhattan and use the mansion as if it was a place to party. And they would come for long weekends. He worked from home, and needed silence. Least of all, he didn't need hangers-on, and he could see that that was what her friends were.

His suggestion that Olivia move into one of the condos he owned, had seemed to be the perfect solution.

It was only with the gift of hindsight that he realized this move was a turning point in their relationship. Everything worsened once she moved to Forest Heights.

He could cook, it wasn't that he couldn't, but he was busy working on deals, and he liked his protein shakes and fruit smoothies. He just didn't have the time to make them up and run the business. He missed Cecile, and he missed her Southern Fried chicken, but it was important for her to be with her sister.

Maybe the new maid could take up the slack? After all, her eggs hadn't been too bad, and she seemed desperate to earn money. Maybe if he asked her nicely enough, she might take him up on the suggestion. She'd been coming and going for the last few days, and he didn't see her as much as he heard her. She was noisier than the last cleaner had been. Vacuuming, and generally whatever she did, she made noise. He'd have to mention it to her.

The sound of the vacuum going in one of the rooms, told him that Jenna was here. He got up and walked towards the noise, only to hear the vacuum suddenly go silent. He found the new maid kneeling on the floor of the living room, examining the underside of the machine.

"Hey," he said, and waited. When she didn't turn to look at him, he cleared his throat, not used to this reaction; not used to someone hearing him and not acknowledging him. "How are you liking it?" he asked a little louder, attempting conversation.

"Liking what?" She pulled something out from the roller, glanced at him, then turned her attention to the roller again.

"The cleaning."

"Great fun." She continued picking apart the vacuum cleaner.

"What are you doing?"

"Cleaning this thing. It hasn't been cleaned in ages. Everything's stuck in the intake port."

"You should have mentioned it." He perched on the armrest of the leather sofa. "I can get you another one."

"It's not *broken*. It needs to be cleaned, that's all."

Making conversation was hard work. "Is there anything else you need?"

"No."

"I wanted to ask you something."

"What?" This time she looked directly at him. He stared at her face, something familiar in those features tugged at him. "I feel like we've met before," he said, unable to shake the notion that he'd seen her somewhere.

"We haven't."

"It's strange, because I feel … you remind me of someone."

"Who?"

"I'm not sure."

She got back to putting the vacuum parts together again. "Then how can I remind you of someone?" She stood up, her finger poised on the button to start the machine again. "What did you want to ask me?"

"I was wondering if you could do a couple of extra hours every day?"

"Extra hours, every day?"

He nodded. "I need someone to make up my fruit smoothies and protein shakes. Is that…is that something you might want to do?" She had pinned her hair so that it was off her face, but he found himself staring at her blue-tipped ends.

She folded her arms. "Are you judging me again?"

He frowned, unsure of what to say because he'd been caught.

"I see you looking at my hair as if you don't know what to think of it."

"I don't know what to think of it," he confessed. "But I'm not judging you."

"How many extra hours?"

"A couple. Whatever you think you need. The fruit smoothies take time, and I'll need you to get the freshest fruit, if you don't mind. I don't have time for these things, and my cook is away, so I'd be grateful if you could do that for now."

She raised an eyebrow, and he couldn't tell if the idea

interested her, or whether she was annoyed by it. Either way, this maid didn't possess the subservient look that he'd come to know and, over time, expect, from the staff that Pennington had hired.

He hoped this new maid would last longer than the last one.

Pennington had ended up firing her after he'd caught her stealing money out of the money jar.

This new maid seemed different. He wasn't used to this; hair that color and a pair of eyes that looked at him coldly. "Cecile, the cook, has a book she uses," he said, "It's on the countertop, a big blue book. Take a look through, and make me a smoothie every time you're here. And there's money in a jar by the toaster. Take what you need for groceries and leave the change and receipts there."

"You don't have to worry about me embezzling money from you. I don't take what isn't mine."

"I'm not the one who'll want to know. Pennington will. He oversees those things and he's away," he said, when Jenna looked at him oddly. "You'll get to meet him eventually. I'll leave you a key near the money jar, so that you can let yourself into the house. With none of my staff here, I don't want to have to get up to answer the door."

She blinked, and he caught the surprise in her eyes. "I'm busy," he replied, feeling as if she was the one who was judging him now.

"I understand."

Only, judging by that expression on her face, he wasn't sure that she did. "So can you do it? The extra hours?"

"Yes. I can. Thanks. Is that all?" Her finger was poised on the button, and by the looks of it, she'd already given him the cue to leave.

He had been about to ask her how long she'd lived in Starling Bay, but she'd turned the vacuum on and he'd lost her attention already.

# CHAPTER 6

She finished vacuuming a couple of the rooms downstairs with a gladness in her heart. A couple of extra hours working here was a godsend, particularly since it wasn't as bad as she had first thought.

Reed stayed out of her way and aside from opening the door to her, she had barely seen him much during the week she had been here. Now that she had a key to let herself in, she would see him even less.

What she did find odd was that she hadn't seen his fiancée yet. After all, it wasn't as if she had a job to go to every day.

The Knight mansion was huge. It was imposing and stately from the outside, and as beautiful on the inside. The rooms had high ceilings and large windows, and there were beautiful stained glass leaded windows in one wing of the house.

It surprised her, that they only had one cleaning person to take care of it all, even with the professional company coming in regularly. Reed had explained that 'the family' as he put it, only occupied one part of the house, and that she was to clean only that part of the house. From that point of view, it was manageable, even for her. She wasn't sure when the cook, someone named Cecile, would be back or when she would meet the butler.

As for her own cleaning duties, Jenna handled a few rooms at a time, and Reed seemed happy with that. He let her get on with it, and he mostly stayed out of her way.

She liked this arrangement. A couple of hours a day cleaning, plus extra time added on for shopping for His Majesty and making his smoothies. She had put up with worse before. She could do this, and despite her initial reservations of returning to the Knight mansion, she couldn't have asked for a better job. It easily beat cleaning offices or the small preschool.

She looped the long vacuum cord around, and was about to walk through to the hallway when she heard the front door open, and then the clackety-clack of stiletto heels on the wooden floor.

"Reed, honey." It was a woman's voice.

"Olivia? What are you doing here?"

"I came over because I got tired of waiting for you."

"Not now. I don't have the time for this. If you want to sulk, Olivia, go ahead, but leave me out of it."

"I wasn't sulking. I was hurt, Reed. We shouldn't be arguing like this."

"You're right. We shouldn't."

"So why don't you apologize, and we can get on with things? Also, I need to talk to you about the ball."

"That goddamn ball," Jenna heard Reed mutter. She paused. The two of them were in the hallway, and she needed to cross it to go into the opposite room. "You're still insisting on going ahead with that thing?"

"It will be fun. *You'll* have fun. You did at the New Year's Eve party, didn't you? And it's *publicity,* Reed. You got a write-up in the local paper for the New Year's Eve party."

Jenna's heart jumped, and she turned her ear towards the door, waiting for Reed's reply. She inched the door open a tiny bit, straining to hear.

"Publicity?" she heard Reed growl. "It's a party. Besides, I don't need publicity."

"Everyone needs publicity."

"You're suddenly eager for it, aren't you?"

"What are you implying?"

There was silence.

Jenna froze, not knowing what she ought to do. This was an embarrassing situation, and she hated being caught up in their argument. But not having laid eyes on Reed's fiancée made her even more curious. She waited with the vacuum cleaner in her hand, unsure of whether to stay in hiding or to boldly make a move to the other rooms she had planned to clean.

"Well?" Olivia asked, when there was still no answer from Reed. Deciding in that instant, Jenna pulled the door open and looked straight ahead at the door across the hall. If she aimed for that then maybe they wouldn't notice her.

"Who's that?" she heard Olivia say.

"The new maid."

With the cord still in her hand and the vacuum following her, Jenna had no choice but to acknowledge Reed's fiancée. "Hello," she said, breezily.

"What happened to the other one?" Olivia asked Reed.

"Pennington fired her."

Olivia laughed. "That man is a darling."

Reed looked as perplexed by her reply as Jenna was. She still stood there as they continued to talk. Olivia hadn't even acknowledged her.

"What did she do?"

"You mean he didn't tell you? I thought Pennington told you everything." The sarcasm in Reed's voice surprised Jenna.

"He didn't mention it. I had no idea she was gone," Olivia said.

"You know nothing about what's going on because you're hardly here. Either you're jetting off to some party, or meeting friends, or you're supposedly looking at exotic faraway honeymoon destinations!"

Jenna was shocked. She'd never heard or seen Reed angry before.

"I know you think I'm partying, but I'm not, darling. We have a lot to do before the wedding," Olivia replied calmly, completely oblivious to Reed's simmering anger. "That's taking up a lot of my time, and don't forget the ball."

Jenna couldn't believe the reply. She quickly glanced at Reed, saw his face turn red and his lips pursed. "*That*'s taking up a lot of your time? And what do you think I'm doing? I have far more serious matters to tend to."

"What happened to your hair?" Olivia asked, as if noticing that Jenna was still here.

She wasn't going to take this lying down. "What happened to yours?" Jenna shot back. Behind her, she saw Reed's eyebrows shoot north.

"Is she allowed to talk to me like that?" Olivia asked Reed.

"It depends. If you don't ask stupid questions, I'm sure Jenna won't either."

She forced herself not to reveal the smile that was about to appear on her lips. Had Reed Knight taken her side against his fiancée's?

Olivia flounced past her and walked up the stairs, announcing, "I'm going to the Hamptons this weekend." Her thin, sculpted, perfect legs turned Jenna green with envy.

"The Hamptons again?" Reed shouted up at her. "I wish you'd go and live there," Jenna heard him mutter in the next moment.

They stared at one another for a split second before Jenna looked away.

"I'd better get back to this." With the vacuum cleaner's cord trailing after her, she disappeared into the room, thankful to be on her own.

But he walked in behind her. "I'm sorry you had to witness that."

"It has nothing to do with me. If you want, I can go and clean the other rooms?" She would be out of earshot then. She felt as if she was caught in enemy fire being here between them both.

"That's not necessary."

He left the room, and a few moments later she heard footsteps and then the door slammed.

Olivia hadn't even said goodbye to Reed or made up with him.

This wasn't the engagement she'd been led to believe. No romance either, from the sounds of it.

Poor man.

For the first time ever, she felt genuinely sorry for Reed Knight.

# CHAPTER 7

*H*is visits to the Blue Velvet Bar were fast becoming his go-to place of relief. He was sitting with Dylan, and they were waiting for Rourke to show up. Reed wiped the condensation off the beer bottle, contemplating the state of things.

"How's Olivia doing?" Dylan asked, freakily intuitive.

"How's Merry?"

"Quick deflection. I asked first."

He ground his teeth together, and that should have told him something.

He felt uneasy with the way things were progressing between him and Olivia. He'd given himself until the New Year's Eve party to make a decision, but she'd come down with a slight cold, and well—he was too much of a gentleman to be that mean. His gut had told him he was making a mistake, yet a part of him kept ignoring the warning signals. He didn't make mistakes. He was a shrewd businessman. He calculated his risk, and his actions were based on carefully thought-out plans.

Except he'd lost his mind with Olivia; he'd lost all reason and logic, and he had proposed not long after meeting her. He spent more time vetting business proposals than he had vetting her. Her acceptance had been instant, and shortly after, she had moved to Starling Bay. And shortly after that, things started to fall apart. Their romance wasn't as easygoing as it had been during that summer month of June in Manhattan.

"She's in The Hamptons."

"Again?"

Quiet anger simmered below the surface. Yes, again. And he didn't even know when she would be back. He wasn't sure he cared much about it, either. The thought smacked into his solar plexus, winding him. If he didn't care, if he felt relief that his fiancée was away, didn't that tell him something?

"Reed?" Dylan asked, when he hadn't replied.

He forced a smile. "Yes, she's gone again. She seems to love that place."

"You might as well buy her a couple of condos over there."

"I already own a couple of condos there."

Dylan shook his head. "I forgot. The Knight empire is everywhere. So what's she doing there this time? Another party?"

"Funny you should say that," he replied, trying to make light of it, except that it wasn't funny. He'd started to see that they had nothing in common. So why was he still continuing with this farce?

Because he didn't like to own up to his mistakes. He didn't like to think he made mistakes. So he tried to remember the Olivia he'd fallen in love with, the one whom he had proposed to at the top of the Empire State Building after their return from St Barts.

"She's going ahead with the ball."

"She is?" asked Dylan, his eyes wide. Reed had mentioned it to the guys in passing a few weeks ago, but he had hoped to put Olivia off the idea. He had failed, of course.

"She's adamant she wants a Valentine's Day Ball."

"Merry will be happy. She loved your New Year's Eve party and wanted me to tell you last time."

Reed smiled. He recalled catching Dylan and Merry wrapped up in one another's arms at the party, away from everyone.

"Tell her she's invited to the Valentine's Day Ball, too." He paused, remembering. "When's she going back to Boston?"

The smile on Dylan's face stretched from ear to ear. "She's not sure yet. Probably never."

Reed gave him a searching look. "You *do* have something to tell me. I should have known that from the start, right from the time you were doing the Christmas pageant."

"It's too soon to make plans."

"Not by the sounds of it." He lifted his bottle in the air, as if proposing a toast. "Congratulations!" He wasn't sure exactly what he was congratulating Dylan for, but his friend seemed happier than he had seen him in years.

"Thanks, but like I said, we're still making plans. It's a big step for Merry. Kind of like how it would have been for Olivia, I guess, when she moved here."

Reed winced. He was certain that Merry had spent more time in Starling Bay than Olivia had. "I'm not so sure we can Olivia a resident of Starling Bay yet."

"You've seen her too?" asked Rourke, suddenly joining them.

"Who are you talking about?" asked Reed.

"Good of you to turn up," said Dylan.

"Sorry. Overran on a meeting. Can we get some more beers in?" Rourke asked, staring at their drinks.

"I was talking about Olivia being a resident of Starling Bay," said Reed dryly. "Who were you talking about?"

"Jenna Lawson."

The name caught Reed's interest, not least because of Jenna, his maid.

"You remember her, she used to go to our school, then left before graduation." Rourke peered at Reed closely.

"I wasn't in your class, and I definitely don't have a clue who you're talking about. Drinks?" asked Dylan, and raised his hand to call the server.

"Jenna Lawson," Rourke repeated, with an excitement that was unusual even for someone like him.

"Lawson?" Reed tried to think, and his brain cells tried to join the dots and make the connection. The new maid hadn't given him her surname, and the name Lawson didn't ring a bell, but... there had been something familiar about her, and the name fit.

"How could you forget her?" Rourke demanded. "It was an evil thing to do, now as I look back upon that time from my misguided youth, but it seemed like fun back then. Remember when those girls turned up to your party, and we didn't let them in?"

Now that Rourke mentioned it, Reed vaguely remembered the incident. "Was she one of *those* girls?"

"Yes! You must have seen her, you couldn't miss her if you tried. She's dyed her hair a crazy blue at the ends. It used to be long before, and dark brown all over. "

Dylan snorted. "Trust you to remember some girl's hair color and style from when you were in your teens. I can't even remember most of the *people* in my class, let alone specific details about them."

"That's because you went to school decades before us," countered Rourke. "Thanks," he said, taking his glass from the server.

"I'm only five years older that you two idiots," Dylan retorted.

But Reed was still in shock. The maid was *that* girl? He hadn't thought about it for years, and even now that Rourke had mentioned it, he didn't remember everything. Except that the idiot group of guys he'd hung around with back then were always daring each other to do stupid things. *"Those girls aren't cool. They're not like us. What did you have to go and invite them for?"* one of his friends had said to him.

"And you say she's got blue hair now?" he asked, slowly as things started to fall into place.

"Yes! She's the one who fell and ripped her skirt."

"I don't remember her falling." What he did remember was his friends bundling him away from the door. One of them had him in a headlock; at his own party, too. *Some friends.* "That's Jenna Lawson?"

"I don't understand how you ended up going to a normal school," Dylan said, picking up a handful of peanuts. "I'd have thought your parents would have sent you away to an insanely expensive boarding school in another state."

"His mom didn't want him to go away to boarding school, even though his dad was eager for him to," Rourke replied.

"So I ended up mixing with the local misfits," Reed stated, but his mind was still trying to piece it all together.

"You didn't turn out so bad, considering," noted Dylan.

But Reed was thinking about the new maid, and this news made him uncomfortable. Now he understood why she had seemed so familiar to him, and he recalled how vehemently she had denied knowing him. He was certain that she hadn't forgotten that incident, and yet she had come back to the Knight mansion to work for him.

She had to be desperate for money.

"I haven't seen her for years," said Reed, curious to know where she had been up until now.

"I told you she left Starling Bay."

"Where did she go?"

"Chicago, I heard. She moved away from here. Imagine, what

you did to her was so traumatic that she was forced to leave the town."

He hadn't even remembered that she'd left. In fact, he couldn't remember much of that time, or that incident. But one thing he was certain of was that it was definitely her. No wonder she had looked familiar. He hadn't been able to see past that blue hair. "She's working for me," he announced.

"What?" Rourke exclaimed. "Are you serious? *She's* working for *you*?"

Reed nodded.

"What did you say when you saw her? What did *she* say?"

"Nothing. I didn't recognize her—even though I thought she seemed familiar—and she didn't bat an eyelid."

"But she must know who you are?" Rourke insisted.

She must have. He was sure of it. She knew she was coming to the Knight mansion.

"That's strange," said Dylan. "She's working right under your nose and you have no clue."

"She has blue hair," he replied, as if that explained everything.

"Is she married?" Rourke asked, his eyes twinkling. "I remember she was cute. Nice big eyes, and a perfect shaped…face."

Reed shrugged.

"He's not looking. He doesn't see these things in other women anymore," Dylan reminded him.

It was true. He hadn't noticed. He wiped his hand over his face at the realization that even this time round, he'd been a total douchebag towards her.

"What did you do?" asked Dylan, picking up on the tell.

"I might have been slightly rude to her when she came to interview for the job. I might have been a little hungover because it was the morning after we met at the Blue Velvet."

"She's been working for you for over a week and you had no

idea?" Rourke lifted his glass to his lips and waited before taking a sip.

"She's changed her hair color, she looks different, familiar but different, and it was a long time ago. I really don't remember turning her away. Are you sure we did that?"

"We did that, maybe not you, but the other idiots."

"Of which you must have been a part," added Reed dryly.

"We were fooling around. It wasn't meant to be nasty."

"I don't remember her and her friends knocking on the door again," Reed retorted. It made him feel bad.

"You can apologize to her if it makes you feel better," said Rourke, jabbing him in the ribs when he didn't answer. "Though you're probably busy with the wedding preparations, huh?"

Reed swallowed, and offered a terse, "Yup."

"When's Olivia coming back?"

He didn't know. She hadn't said, and they hadn't called one another. "In a couple of days."

"I can't see how you guys get to spend much time together with her living at her condo—"

"At my condo," Reed interjected.

"Whatever," said Rourke, barely pausing to draw breath. "With you both living in separate places and her being away so much."

The muscles along Reed's jaw tightened, and he could feel Dylan staring at him. "It works for us," he said, lifting his beer bottle. Then, because he was desperate to change the subject, he told Rourke, "We're having a Valentine's Day Ball."

Rourke rubbed his hands together, like a kid gearing up to make trouble. "It's definitely going ahead?"

"Definitely."

"Who's on the guest list?" he asked, his eyes lighting up like fireworks.

"Damned if I know," replied Reed.

# CHAPTER 8

He'd been working for hours and liked it when he could do that without interruption. A quiet house and no drama made for a good day.

Jenna made noise, when she worked, but it was more like white noise, in the background and easy to ignore.

Come to think of it, she hadn't made him a smoothie today either. She usually knocked on the door and told him when she had. He hadn't heard her today, nor had he heard the sound of the vacuum going, or the usual clanging and clacking of mops and cleaning equipment. He hadn't even heard her going up or down the stairs.

The house was eerily silent.

Puzzled, he walked around the rooms with his cell phone in one hand and a leather binder in the other, so that he looked busy. So that she wouldn't think he was checking up on her.

But she was nowhere to be found; at least, she wasn't in any of the rooms downstairs. Now he was more than a little curious. He walked around the kitchen and the different living rooms, and then finally went upstairs and started looking through the rooms up there.

Had she even come today?

And then he walked into his bedroom and found her. His eyes widened in disbelief. She was lying on the bed. On *his* bed, fast asleep. Almost like Goldilocks, only with blue hair and a duster in her hand.

He stepped back, quietly surprised. Now that he could examine her face, it all came back to him. That was the face that closely resembled the girl from his high school days; he had a vague recollection of a girl at school that he had helped up from the track once. It might have been her. He thought it was her, but he wasn't sure. It was so long ago.

Watching her now, he didn't know what to do—whether he should wake her or not. Wake her for what? To tell her to get back to cleaning?

He couldn't do that.

It was cold and almost coming up to early evening; the time she would normally be finishing up. He wanted to put a blanket over her, but decided not to, in case it woke her up.

Quiet as a mouse, he tiptoed out of the room and closed the door behind him.

It was the loud voices which woke her up, and as she opened her eyes, she realized that she was in bed. But it wasn't *her* bed.

She jolted upright and sprang off the bed so fast she almost tripped. As the duster fell to the floor, she realized that she'd been sleeping in Reed Knight's bed. She steadied herself against the dresser in shock. A glance at her wristwatch told her that it was nearly nine o'clock; the time when she should have been back at home. She should have finished cleaning a few hours ago.

How would she explain herself to Reed? Did he even know she was still here?

*His smoothie.* She put her hand to her brow. She hadn't made it.

He would have been waiting for it and probably wondering why she hadn't made it today.

It was better to go downstairs and own up, to tell him that she had fallen asleep, and would come back tomorrow because it was too late for her to be doing anything now. Juggling three jobs was getting to be too much, especially with the extra hours Reed had asked her to do, but she needed the money. She'd already insisted to Shay that she could handle it and she would have to.

But as she opened the door to tiptoe downstairs, she heard Olivia's voice.

Her blood froze.

Olivia was back.

The last thing Jenna needed was for Reed's fiancée to come charging into his bedroom and find *her* here. But before she could concoct a plan and a suitable explanation, the voices got louder. They were directly below the landing, at the foot of the stairs, and their voices carried clearly upwards.

"It's a photo shoot, Reed. A one-day photo shoot. It will tie in nicely with the Valentine's Day Ball."

"Tie in nicely? You have nerve, Olivia. You've been gone for days, and now you waltz back in here and casually announce that some fashion magazine wants to do a photo shoot here. This is my house. I live and work here. I'm a busy man, and I have a lot of pressure. I have a lot of things to juggle, and take care of. The last thing I need is for a human circus to set up camp here. for a photo shoot I neither want nor care about."

"But, but I thought…"

"You thought what?"

"We're engaged to be married. I thought it would be…"

"You really don't see how selfish you're being?"

"Selfish, me?"

Jenna flinched at the note of surprise in Olivia's voice. "Darling, I've been working hard trying to convince one of the best photographers in Manhattan to come here. I can't get him for the wedding but—"

She heard a THWACK, as if he'd punched something hard.

"Enough, Olivia."

"It's a good thing that door is made of oak," said Olivia.

Jenna held her breath, not daring to breathe. Reed's fiancée didn't seem to care. And as for Reed, the man had a real temper on him, and one that Olivia seemed adept at drawing out.

"What's wrong with you?" Olivia's voice rose an octave. "I've never seen you like this before. You're nothing like the man I fell in love with."

"And you're nothing like the woman I fell in love with."

"Most men would die to be with a woman like me."

"Most men would die *if* they ended up with a woman like you."

"You don't mean that!" cried Olivia sounding distressed.

Jenna clutched her hand to her heart. She was always in the wrong place at the wrong time. This was not only insane, her overhearing this, it was dangerous. All these two ever seemed to do was argue. Theirs was a match made in hell, even if it looked like a fairytale romance from outside.

"I *do* mean that. You're like a different person, Olivia. I don't know who you are anymore."

"It's still me, baby," Olivia's voice softened. "It's still me. I'm overwhelmed. This takes some getting used to, being here."

"You're never here," he snapped.

"That's because I don't want to get in your way. You work from home and—"

"And you're too busy partying. I can't believe you've waltzed here after all these days, thinking everything was fine. No phone call, no text message, no email, and the first thing you tell me about is the photo shoot. That isn't what a relationship should be like. We don't have a relationship."

"That's not true!"

"We don't have a lot in common, admit it."

Jenna peeked her head out of the door, trying to hear, since their voices had gotten lower. Reed sounded resigned, sad almost.

"Of course we do."

"No, Olivia, we don't. I've been thinking about it a lot and I think we made a mistake."

"A mistake?"

"I'm not sure we're right for one another."

"You're the only man for me."

"That's not true. You can't say that and behave the way you do."

"Behave the way I do? What are you talking about?"

"I honestly think we rushed into things, and I think...I think...I think this isn't working anymore."

"Are you breaking up with me?"

"I've been thinking a lot about things lately, and I think we both know that things aren't working out for—"

"But I love you!" Olivia's shrill cry floated up the stairs. It was the sound of a woman desperate to hold onto something.

"I don't want to hurt you, Olivia, but this isn't working out. We should have taken things slowly. I made a hasty decision—"

"A hasty decision? No, you didn't, Reed. You're overworked, and overwhelmed, you're getting frustrated by everything."

"It not as simple as frustration, trust me. I've thought about this for a while now. We're not how we used to be, and the more I think about it, we're completely different people. It would be a mistake to go forward."

She heard an anguished cry from Olivia. "You *are* breaking up with me."

With her heart stuck in her throat, Jenna waited for Reed's

answer, but all she heard were the clackety-clack sounds of Olivia's stilettoes on wood.

And then the sound of the door slamming.

Jenna retreated into the room, anxious not to be found out. She couldn't go downstairs now. It would be too obvious that she had heard. She stood there, her heart beating as if she'd done an aerobics class, and she waited out ten, twenty, thirty minutes, listening out for the sound of Reed's footsteps in case he came upstairs.

Each minute seemed to stretch out for longer, but she forced herself to stay put for another ten minutes in order to make it look seem that she had fallen into a deep sleep.

When she did finally come downstairs, it was to find Reed sitting in the kitchen, staring at his cellphone. She caught sight of photos of him and Olivia, before he looked up at her and quickly put the phone away.

She didn't know what to say. He looked so lost, so defeated. "I have a confession to make," she said, standing on the opposite end of the kitchen island.

He blinked, but said nothing.

"I fell asleep." Honesty seemed like the best way to go about this. He looked the most disheveled she had ever seen him. His dirty blond hair was roughed up, and he looked as if he hadn't slept in days.

"Sleep well?" he asked, his expression blank.

What could she say? That she had slept like a two-week-old puppy in front of a cozy fire, and had then woken up and heard everything. She could have explained more, but seeing him like this made her hesitate, especially after having heard all that she had. For the first time ever, she was flustered. "It's a comfortable bed," she said, scratching her head.

"I figured you must have liked it."

"You saw me?" The knowledge that he had doubly mortified her.

He looked apologetic. "I needed to get something from my room. I didn't mean to walk in on you."

"Don't apologize. It's your room. I shouldn't have fallen asleep in it."

His cell phone beeped, and he stared at it. She wondered if it was Olivia, going crazy texting him.

She looked over at the fruit bowl. "I'll make you a shake."

"Don't worry about it now."

"I can make you a shake." It's the least she could do, because he looked so defeated.

"Don't bother."

She wasn't going to push it.

"Did you just wake up now?" he asked. She could tell he was fishing, that he was trying to find out if she had heard anything.

She pretend-yawned. "I must have been in a deep sleep," she said. Then lied, in an effort to convince him further. "My phone went off plenty of times and I never even heard it."

"Everything okay?"

"It was my roommate calling to see where I was."

"She must worry about you and that ancient bike. I'm surprised that thing hasn't fallen apart."

"It helps me get around. She was worried because I'm never this late getting back. I'm really sorry about what happened today."

He waved his hand, dismissing her concerns, and a flurry of pings went off on his phone. More texts, she guessed. He turned his cell phone off.

"Can I make up for it tomorrow?"

"Sure."

"Your hand," she cried, noticing the knuckles all red and grazed and looking swollen. It looked bad.

"It's nothing."

"That doesn't look like nothing," she said, rushing to the refrigerator and getting some ice.

"It's fine. I—I had a slight accident."

"What happened?" she asked, as she wrapped the ice-cubes in a dry dishcloth.

"You don't have to do that," he said, then winced as she placed the compress on his knuckles. He wasn't going to give her an answer.

"Some accident," she said.

"Yeah."

"Keep that pressed," she told him. "It should help take the swelling down."

"Thanks."

"I'll come a little early tomorrow to make up my hours."

"Okay, if that suits you."

She cycled home thinking that Reed Knight had many sides. In recent days she had started to agree with Shay, that the guy wasn't so bad after all. He had seemed like a typical rich guy, that first day she had turned up here, but the more she was around him, the more she came to see that he was pretty normal.

So normal, that she'd been moved to take a look at his bloody hand. Strange, how much her opinion of him had changed in such a short amount of time.

# CHAPTER 9

"*Y*ou fell asleep?" Shay asked.

"I fell asleep." Jenna collapsed on the sofa alongside Shay and dipped her hand into the bowl of popcorn resting on her friend's lap.

"Don't tell me you feel asleep on Reed Knight's bed," said Shay, planting the bowl on Jenna's lap.

"Okay, then. I won't."

"You fell asleep on his bed? Are you nuts?"

"I was tired." Jenna grabbed a handful of popcorn.

"I knew it would be too much, juggling three different jobs. I shouldn't have let you talk me into giving them to you."

"I won't fall asleep again. I promise."

"But can you handle it, Jenna? Can your body handle it?"

"Yes!" She needed to build up her savings supply, and start to get herself back on her feet. "I've been sleeping in your apartment and getting in your way—"

"I never said you were in my way," Shay insisted.

"I'm grateful to you for letting me stay, but it could be a while before I'm able to rent a place of my own." She hated this the most, not being able to tell her friend when she would leave. She had no timeframe for it.

"Don't worry," Shay said cheerfully. "It's nice having you around."

"You say that now, but you won't next month."

Shay rolled her eyes, and dunked her hand into the popcorn bowl. "You worry too much."

"I worry about money and never having enough."

"That's called a self-fulfilling prophecy."

"It seems to be the story of my life." She was sick of being dirt poor. Things had been hard enough in Chicago, but she'd been seriously deluded into thinking things would be easier in Starling Bay. The place had changed so much from when she had lived here before. Back then, as a teenager, she hadn't had to worry about paying the rent and getting by. Life just seemed so much harder the older she got.

Why did she make such poor choices in life? Her friends seemed to be doing well enough. Even Roxy, someone she had known from school, was running her own diner. And Shay had a good job working for a recruitment company. Why was she the only one who always seemed to struggle?

"Then maybe it's time for you to rewrite the story of your life."

"I'm trying to. That's why I'm working all these jobs."

"You're not supposed to fall asleep on your boss's bed. I'm surprised he hasn't fired you."

"He can't fire me, he has no one else to make his smoothies." The poor man was always working or dealing with Olivia's outbursts. She felt sorry for the man, and sorry wasn't something she ever thought she'd feel for him.

"Hasn't he recognized you yet?"

"Not yet." He seemed like a man who had other more pressing issues consuming him. Overhearing that argument had been eye-opening. Some lives looked gilded from afar, but on closer inspection were still caked with muck. "Plus, I don't see him much," she confessed.

"That's because you're fast asleep on his bed!" Shay chortled uncontrollably, then gasped. "What if his fiancée has seen you? You're lucky she didn't. That would have been difficult to explain."

"She's not really there much, though she turned up this evening. It sounds as if she's in New York most of the time," Jenna told her.

"I've heard that, too. What is she like?" Shay asked.

"I've only seen her a couple of times." And both of those times she and Reed didn't seem to get along. "They seem to argue a lot."

"Do they?" asked Shay, her voice turning all sweet and tell-me-more-ish. "What do they argue about?"

"I have no idea. I don't hear it, because I'm usually in the other room, vacuuming or doing something."

"I can't imagine Miss Wisconsin liking it too much around here. I wondered if she would feel like a fish out of water when she moved to Starling Bay."

As far as Jenna could tell, she did. It was there on the tip of her tongue to tell Shay the news—that Reed and Olivia weren't getting along and it seemed as if they were splitting up. But she decided against it. Though she had no loyalty towards Reed, it didn't feel right telling her friend something that wasn't common knowledge yet.

# CHAPTER 10

*E*ven if his feelings towards Olivia had changed, he still cared about her, and the fact that she hadn't answered her cell phone worried him.

Reed set off towards Forest Heights, assuming that Olivia was still here and hadn't jetted off to New York again. Maybe they had a communication problem? Maybe it was taking time for her to settle into Starling Bay. Maybe it was a whole heap of things and he hadn't been there for her?

Maybe they just weren't right for each other.

He parked in the parking lot and drew out a long exhale. If he walked in, she would think he still cared, worse, that he'd changed his mind. And he hadn't. He'd meant what he'd said yesterday.

He should have done this a long, long time ago.

Or rather, he should *never* have gotten engaged. The change in her personality had been so fast, so shocking, it was almost a 180-degree turnaround, and it had taken him by surprise.

People would talk when they found out, but he wasn't worried about what people would say, or the rumor that would spread around the town like a brush fire. People talked even when there was no story to entertain them. He had to prepare for the fallout and move on. In a year's time, if not sooner, he would see that he had done the right thing. Of course his parents would have a hard time understanding. His father loved Olivia. He thought she was perfect daughter-in-law material. His mother hadn't been so enthralled on hearing about his sudden engagement. She'd asked Reed if he'd thought things through, if he knew Olivia well enough before making such a life-changing decision. He should have taken heed then.

Well, at least he had made another life-changing decision yesterday. He braced himself as he got out of the car and walked towards Olivia's apartment.

At first, he was tempted to go in. He had the key. It was his apartment, after all, but chivalry stopped him. For now, Olivia lived here, and it was her place. So he rang the doorbell. When there was no answer, he let himself in. What he didn't expect was to find a guy sitting on his couch, with headphones on, watching something on his iPad.

"Who the hell are you?" he yelled so loudly that the man turned and ripped off his headphones.

"Who are you?" the stranger shrieked, clearly terrified as he shot off the couch. The iPad dropped onto the rug.

"I'm Marc. Olivia invited me over."

Reed clenched his fists, needing to smack the wall, the door, any surface that was hard. "She invited you?" he bellowed, stepping towards the man, his cold gaze running up and down his body. "You're in your boxer briefs," he thundered. Blood boiled inside him.

"Calm down, I slept on the couch."

*Calm down?* He was going to spontaneously combust if he had to stand here any longer. "Olivia!" he blared at the top of his lungs.

A door rattled somewhere and hurried footsteps rushed

towards him. "What in the—" Her terrified expression told him he'd surprised her. "What are you doing here?"

"What's he doing here?" he nodded at the guy.

She had the audacity not to blush, or looked embarrassed, or look guilty. "He stayed over. He's from the fashion magazine, the ones who are doing the photo shoot. They sent him over to come and check out the mansion and...we were going to come over later today so I could show him around the mansion."

He shook his head. She was calm and rational and talking as if everything was normal—as if this guy being here in his boxer briefs was normal, while she took a shower. And she was still talking about the damned photo shoot.

*Had she been cheating on him?*

"What's he doing here, Olivia?"

"He slept over."

"You expect me to believe that?"

"Yes! Nothing's going on, Reed."

"Yeah, man. I slept on the couch. Look." The stranger pointed to the couch and the blanket, as if he were a toddler and it was his security blanket.

Reed glared at Olivia. "Are you cheating on me?"

"Of course not!"

Olivia sidled up to him. "Reed," her voice was apologetic, and with a softness it had back when they had first met. "Nothing happened. If I was going to do something, do you think I'd be stupid enough to do it here in Starling Bay?"

"No, Olivia, I'd expect you to fly off to Manhattan and do it there."

"You can be so nasty," she shot back.

"Some people would think I'm fairly restrained, given the circumstances." He threw the guy a sidelong glance then looked back at Olivia. "I came because I was worried about you, and look what I found instead."

"You were worried?" Olivia asked.

"I don't care anymore."

"Nothing happened!"

"Nothing happened," the man echoed. "Like I said, I came over because—"

"What kind of fashion magazine do you work for that can't afford to pay your overnight stay in a hotel?"

They both stared at him in silence.

"We got talking and—"

"I'm done," said Reed, his stomach twisting as if he'd been knifed.

"Done? What do you mean you're done?" Olivia cried, her voice bordering on hysterical.

He was sick of listening to Olivia's lies and explanations. He marched towards the door, not wanting to hear any more. He couldn't stomach being here, and so, he stormed out, because there wasn't much else to say.

He walked out of the condo, feeling as if he was disintegrating, as if his insides were slowly turning to mush. She didn't come after him. As he headed back towards his car he thought he heard someone call out his name.

"Reed!" He turned to look. A man in the distance waved at him. By his side was a dog that looked as big as a pony. "Reed!" he repeated, when Reed looked confused. It was only when the man started to walk towards him that he realized it was Dylan.

But Reed wasn't in the mood to talk to anyone right now, least of all Dylan. The guy could see through him. In fact, Reed was certain that his friend was onto him.

"Hey," he said, "What are you doing walking that Baby Elephant of yours?"

Dylan snorted. "Meet Spart."

"Spart?" Reed asked, looking warily at the beast. The temporary distraction was a welcome relief.

"Spartacus. Merry's dog."

"So this is the infamous creature." Dylan had told them how this dog had brought him and Merry together. "You're walking him?" Dylan's store was nearby, and it seemed that he and Merry were spending a lot of time together.

"Merry wanted to show Chloe one of the one-story houses. Apartments aren't ideal for a dog."

"So she is moving here?" Reed asked.

"She's thinking about it."

"She's more than thinking about it if she's looking at houses to buy."

"She's just looking," Dylan insisted.

"Sounds serious."

Dylan looked at him with a slight smile dancing on his lips. "It might be heading that way. I love having her around."

"Yeah?" Reed asked, knowing that he didn't feel this way about Olivia, not anymore.

"I feel as if I've known her all my life."

"All your life?"

"It's weird, but yeah. I can't imagine not having her in my life. You feel the same, right?"

Reed couldn't answer that question truthfully, and definitely not out loud. "You two moved pretty fast," he said, instead.

"As if you and Olivia didn't. The summer in Manhattan did things to you, Reed."

"Yeah," he said, making the mental comparison. Dylan and Merry's romance had blossomed right under his nose. One moment Dylan had been single, the next moment, he was with Merry. Seeing the two of them together he could see how right they were for one another.

He and Olivia weren't, and what he had seen at the apartment just now had convinced him of that. He couldn't be sure something went on, and even if it didn't, he felt uneasy seeing a guy at her apartment in his boxer briefs. Would Olivia have been able to say the same if the tables had been turned?

He'd gone to check up on her with the best of intentions, but he'd come back convinced that they were done.

"So what's next?"

"We're not getting engaged or anything," Dylan said quickly. "There are so many things to think about, especially with regards to Chloe. We don't want to rush into anything but, I have to say, she lights up my world."

"Lights up your world," Reed echoed. "That's what you want." He hoped one day he would be able to say that. As things stood at present, his immediate future was bleak. He'd lost his head with the ex-beauty queen, and now he was suffering the consequences. Still, calling off the engagement was better than getting divorced. He didn't want to think about how they were going to manage the announcement. Didn't want to think about it, after the kick to his gut just now.

"What are you doing here?" Dylan asked. The question momentarily stumped him.

"I…uh…I came to see Olivia."

Dylan said nothing, but looked at him a while longer than necessary.

"I need to get back," Reed said, putting his hand out. "Got a few deals to sign off on."

"Said like a true businessman," Dylan replied, shaking his hand hard. "You're looking rough. Did you forget to shave?"

"You know how it is when I get busy."

"You know where I am, if you need to talk."

# CHAPTER 11

She tried to act normal around him, but knowing what she did, it wasn't easy. Jenna couldn't help but feel sorry for Reed but as before, she didn't see him much. He remained buried in his study for long stretches of time.

She'd seen his half-eaten deli sandwiches lying around. They didn't look appetizing, and so one morning, she picked up some olive bread rolls and roast chicken slices, and made him a couple of rolls with the avocado leftover from his smoothie. She left them next to the smoothie in the kitchen, knocked on his door to tell him she'd made his smoothie, then went off to do her daily cleaning chores.

She'd been working on the toilet, scrubbing away at the bowl when he happened by a short while later. His casual knock on the door made her jump with fright.

"You scared me!" She gasped and glanced over her shoulder, her hand still on the toilet brush which was still inside the basin.

"Sorry," he said. "I was out, I got back a while ago."

"You were out? I didn't even know."

"I went over to see my fian—" he stopped short. "I went out." He rubbed a hand over his jaw and she could see that he hadn't shaved in days. "I knocked on your door to tell you I'd made your smoothie."

"Thanks. Were those sandwich rolls for me, the ones next to the smoothie?"

"Well, they weren't for me."

"Good, because I finished them."

"Great."

"Thanks. They were delicious."

"You're welcome." She expected him to leave, but he didn't, instead he stood there as if he had more to say. "What?" she asked, waiting for the bombshell. "Did I do something wrong?"

"No, no. I only came to thank you for the food, and to make sure you hadn't fallen asleep again."

He smiled and his attempt at a joke made her avert her gaze, because that event embarrassed her, even if it seemed to amuse him. "That won't happen again."

"I hope it doesn't, for your sake, especially when Pennington's around. He's back tomorrow." He shrugged. "He runs the place."

"Should I be afraid?" She wondered what the butler was like.

Reed laughed. "It depends. He doesn't suffer fools gladly, so I think you'll be fine. Just don't fall asleep. He fired the last cleaner because she stole from the money jar."

"Ah." The man obviously believed he was at the top of the food chain. She'd better watch out, but she had nothing to hide. She was honest and a hard worker, and she wouldn't fall asleep again. "It won't happen again on this shift."

"This shift?" he asked, curious. "Are you working somewhere else as well?"

She pressed her lips together, not eager to explain, but not wanting to lie either. If he'd wanted to fire her, he would have done so that day she'd fallen asleep on his bed. "I won't be able to buy my palace just by working here," she replied truthfully.

"If you needed more hours, you should have said…"

"You gave me more hours."

"If you want any more, let me—"

"I've got the other jobs," she said, cutting him off. He was feeling sorry for her, and she didn't want that, not from him. He'd been born into money, and most people weren't. But she kept her thoughts to herself.

"Oh?" he asked, expressing an interest. "Where else are you working?"

She explained, telling him about the offices she cleaned early in the morning before most people woke up, and how, after that, she then went onto the small preschool after that. And how, after cleaning that, she returned home by breakfast time, the time most people would be leaving to start work at the office. After napping, and showering, and puttering around, she would cycle to the Knight mansion in the afternoon.

"I noticed the bike," he said. She left it propped up against one of the side walls of the mansion. "It's not mine. It's my… friend's." She was about to mention Shay, but he hadn't reacted to mention of her name when she had turned up that first day for her interview. Clearly, he had forgotten most of his peers from school. She and Shay were nobodies.

"Three jobs is a lot." He sounded impressed.

"Someone's got to do it."

"You're right, someone does, and it may as well be you." He seemed to be looking for something else to say, and she waited, expectantly, and politely. Until he said, "By the way, you've changed my opinion of avocados."

That surprised her. Was this a compliment? "I had leftover avocado from your smoothies, so I threw it into the bread roll."

"Threw," he muttered, "Interesting choice of word."

"I didn't spit in it, though," she said, and then wondered, as the words left her lips, if the guy could take a joke.

His lips curled upwards. "How considerate of you."

If she was trying to suppress a smile, she had failed. He *could* take a joke. Maybe he wasn't as stuck up as she'd thought.

As for making him rolls, she'd done that out of pity. He didn't know that she knew about him and Olivia; he didn't know she felt sorry for him.

"It's no big deal, really," she said, and started scrubbing the toilet again.

"It is for me," he said, surprising her. By the time she turned around, he'd already disappeared.

# CHAPTER 12

He hid away in his study, working long hours, keeping himself busy. Jenna made him a light snack every day; it was either a sandwich or a roll, and a couple of times she even asked him if he wanted her to make something light and easy for his evening meal. He politely declined, but was touched by her thoughtfulness; he couldn't remember Olivia ever making him a sandwich, let alone a smoothie. Come to think of it, Olivia had never asked him if he needed anything.

When his parents called, asking him how the wedding arrangements were going and whether he and Olivia had settled on a honeymoon destination yet, he changed the subject. While he wanted to hint to them that they were having problems, he couldn't find it in himself to do so, not over the phone. He didn't want to lie to them, either, and tell them that everything was fine.

He would have to break the real news to them in person, and once these next few events were over with, he planned to take time out and make a trip to Montana.

Besides, he had yet to discuss with Olivia how they would break the news. It made him feel like a failure, to know that things had reached this point, and were unsalvageable—as far as he was concerned—but he was convinced it was the right thing to do, to break up, and move on. It gave him a feeling of relief.

Pennington had returned late last night. His living quarters were at the other end of the house, and it wasn't until Reed had gone into the kitchen earlier this morning to make his morning coffee that he had seen him and heard all about his trip to Costa Rica.

Reed was more concerned about how Pennington and Jenna would get on. Later that afternoon he took his laptop into the kitchen to catch up with some emails, and to be around to make introductions when Jenna arrived.

"When is Cecile due back?" Pennington asked.

"She's not sure yet. She called to say her sister's still not steady on her crutches and she doesn't want to leave her."

"I understand that her sister had a knee replacement," replied his butler, "In which case she could be gone a while. I'm going to get in a temporary cook until then."

"Jenna's already taking care of it."

Pennington raised a silver eyebrow. "She's cleaning *and* cooking?"

"It's simple stuff. Doesn't take long. She fixes me a light lunch, but it's way after lunchtime because she doesn't start until late afternoon."

"Late afternoon? Why?"

"Because it suits her."

"She needs to do what suits you."

"It suits me too," Reed replied, easily. "Stick around, she'll be here soon and I'll introduce you both."

"I assume you and Miss Sykes are still dining out in the evenings?"

Reed sat forward, and reached for his glass of fruit juice. "Not lately, no. It's been a busy couple of weeks and I haven't seen much of her." He wasn't ready to tell Pennington about their breakup yet. He wasn't ready to tell anyone. It was something he wanted to avoid altogether, because it was a sign of something he had gotten wrong, a situation he had misjudged. A mistake, and he wasn't ready to own up to those things right now.

"Ah," was Pennington's reply. Reed turned at the sound of soft footsteps in the hallway. He'd been waiting for Jenna to arrive so that he could introduce the two of them. He'd been anticipating her arrival.

"Why are you working here today?" Pennington asked, looking at the laptop which lay on the table.

"Because I needed a change of environment." And because he was waiting for Jenna to arrive.

"Of course."

The sound of Jenna talking made them both turn to the door. She walked in, talking to someone on her cell phone. "Gotta go, bye." She looked surprised. "What's this?" she asked him. "How come you're in the kitchen?"

"Turns out my being in the kitchen at this time of day is a huge shock to both of you," said Reed. "I was waiting for you to arrive. This is Jenna," he told Pennington. To Jenna, he said, "Meet Pennington."

"She has a key?" Pennington asked him.

"Yes, she has a key." What a thing to ask. At times, his butler could be overly patronizing. "You weren't around, and I didn't want to have to answer the door."

"But after the last maid?"

"Pennington. I can vouch for Jenna." He didn't want to explain it now, that he knew who she was, and that he couldn't see her stealing from the money jar. Jenna had done nothing shady. If anything, she had shown him more care and understanding than his own fiancée had.

"But the last maid stole from—"

"That's enough." He could sense Jenna's unease, and was

aware that she was still hovering by the door, and that she hadn't ventured in.

He got up, seeing that the introduction had been a shambles, and picked up his laptop, ready to return back to his study, away from the drama. But the sound of stilettoes on the wooden floor signaled Olivia's arrival. Now *there* was someone whose key he needed to claim back.

She strode into the kitchen, and, seeing Pennington, rushed towards him in delight. "Pennington!" she exclaimed. "How lovely to see you again. When did you get back?"

Reed stared at her, wondering what she was doing here, and wondered if she'd been waiting for his butler to get back.

He walked towards the door, towards Jenna who still stood there with her phone still in her hand.

"I wanted you to meet my butler," he said, feeling the need to explain.

"Consider him met."

"He's not so bad, when you get to know him," Reed whispered. "He's one of the old guard, he likes to think there's a hierarchy in place here."

"Isn't that what all the Knights believe?" she quipped.

"No, not all of us."

"May I speak to you in private?" It was Olivia, and she looked timid; something that didn't suit her expression.

"In my study," he said, needing to speak to her too.

Jenna was about to walk into the kitchen, probably to make his food, but she turned around and disappeared into the utility room. He had often wondered when might be the right time to bring up the topic, for him to tell her that he knew who she was, for he was most curious to see her reaction, but the timing for them to have that conversation never seemed right.

He led Olivia through to his study, his initial irritation at her appearance disappearing. It was better to get this conversation over with.

"Thank you for seeing me," she said, as she closed the door.

He turned to face her. "I'm glad you want to talk. We need to discuss how we're going to manage this."

She looked confused, as if he'd said something she hadn't been expecting. "I...I wanted to explain the situation the other day—"

He blinked in surprised. "There's nothing to explain. I saw it all with my eyes, Olivia. There's nothing that can be explained away."

"But you're jumping to the wrong conclusion."

"Am I?"

"Yes! Nothing happened."

"Even if I hadn't seen that, I still would have reached the same conclusion."

"About what?" she asked.

"About us not being right for each other."

She stepped towards him and lifted her hands to his chest.

"Don't touch me, Olivia," he warned her. She pulled away as if she'd touched fire.

"Marc is a photographer. There was nothing going on."

"And yet he was in your apartment in just his boxer briefs, while you were in the shower?"

"He stayed over, we got talking and it was late."

"And he couldn't get a cab to a hotel?"

"It was nothing."

"What *we* have is nothing. It's not just that one incident, Olivia. Things between us aren't working."

"They *can* work."

"We want different things."

"We can start to appreciate one another's different personalities."

"I don't think I can."

"You have to understand, Reed, it's not been easy for me, trying to settle in Starling Bay. This is such a small town, and I'm not used to it, not after being in New York for so many years."

"You're from a small town in Wisconsin," he reminded her.

"There's nothing here for me."

"There is for me."

"I need time."

"It's not about the location, Olivia, or the length of time you think you need in order to feel settled here. It goes deeper than that, and now that I've had time to think about things, I can see that I've been in denial for months."

"In denial? For months?"

He nodded. "I think you know deep down that the spark we had when we first met hasn't been enough to sustain us." Her eyes welled up as he continued. "It won't be easy, breaking the news to everyone, that's why I wanted to talk to you. My parents keep asking me about the wedding. We'll have to let people know soon."

"You mean to say that this is it? That we are over?"

He knew she would turn it around, pretend that he was over-exaggerating, that she hadn't heard or understood him at her condo the other day. He expected her denial, and he was prepared. "You haven't heard a word I've said to you since the other day."

"This is it?" she asked again. "You're actually breaking up with me?"

"Yes."

Her eyes turned glassy and moist, and he felt a touch of pity for her, but his empathy didn't last long, because her next words would shock the hell out of him. "Then at least let me have the Valentine's Day Ball."

He blinked, and blinked again. "The Valentine's Day Ball?" he asked, shocked. Was that why she had come to see him today?

"Please, Reed."

She was concerned about the Valentine's Day Ball, and concerned about taking, taking, taking. Spending his money for one final big party, for something he cared nothing about. Her priorities were nothing like his. He had been truly blinded by her beauty, and now, seeing her beg like this, made his stomach churn.

"And the photo shoot."

The insides of his stomach almost emptied to the floor. "The photo shoot?"

She still wanted to go ahead with the photo shoot and the ball. He could not have been more wrong about anything or anyone in his entire life.

"You don't understand," she said, holding back tears.

"You're right. I don't understand." It would have to take Rourke and Dylan and a night of beers for him to get his head around this. "You want to go ahead with the ball and the photo shoot, even though I've told you that we are not compatible, and that we are splitting up, and that I made a mistake. You were the mistake I made, Olivia. Do you not get that? And yet you still want to go ahead with those things?" Why were they so important to her? Was she holding onto that idea of romance because she couldn't bear to part with it?

"You don't know what it's like," she said. "To be poor and to have nothing."

"You were Miss Wisconsin, you can't say you had nothing." He thought of how that might have been the pinnacle of her career, of her life even, being crowned and handed flowers to the sound of cheers and applause. She had probably been pining to relive that that moment ever since.

"Years ago, I was someone. I achieved success, you might laugh at it because it's not your definition of success, but it was mine. And then...and then..."

He could see the muscles on either side of her cheek flex as she struggled to keep her composure.

"And then?" he asked, softly, even though he understood it now. Her being with him had given her opportunities. That's what the Valentine's Day Ball and the photo shoot were about. Her stab at a new opportunity. That was all he had been for her, all along. She wasn't upset that their engagement was off, she was upset because of the things she would no longer have access to now that they weren't together. He could see her finding someone else to take his place. Not someone like that photographer in her condo, but someone with money, status, and power.

"And now I'm nobody. You don't understand because you've been someone your whole life. You're rich, and important, and people respect you."

"I haven't craved respect, Olivia, and I can't help that I'm rich, but I certainly don't consider myself as someone important. Important for whom? For what?"

She laughed. "That's because it's a given. People treat you differently because of who you are, because of what you were born into."

"It's not my fault I was born into wealth."

"It's not my fault I'm trying to make something of my life in the only way I know how." Her face hardened. "You don't even need to work, Reed. You have other people working for you."

"I still need to keep the businesses going. I still need to earn my keep. You think I don't have any worries? You think all of this is easy?"

"But you had a head start. You don't even know how lucky you are. Please, Reed. Please let me have this. I've finally found a way to get my career back on track. This could be huge for me."

"A ball?"

"The photo shoot. I'll get exposure. I might get noticed."

"Did you ever love me?" he asked. She tried to put her hands on his shoulders, but he held out his hand, palm facing her, halting her. "Stop. I don't want or need your melodrama."

She stopped, but her face crumpled. "I love you. I do love you. I love you even now. It's not me that's changed. It's you."

"Wrong. *You've* changed, and the fact that you can't see it makes me wonder how I could have gotten things so wrong."

He'd moved fast without thinking, had lost his mind for a crazy few weeks in the summer. Her beauty had turned his head, and he'd fallen for her, but it wasn't too late for him to back out and do it favorably. She was now giving him the chance, and he didn't want a scandal.

The Knight name was blemish-free, and he was a man who didn't court publicity, nor desired attention. If he gave her what she wanted, and they got to go their separate ways, he considered that a win.

He could move on, explain to his parents and his friends and put this all behind him. The news would make headlines in Starling Bay for a few days and then disappear.

It would be better to give in to her demands, and give her the chance to walk away with something—even if it was only the fragile promise of a resurrected career. Olivia was right. Maybe he had taken his inherited wealth, and his luck at being born a Knight, for granted. He only had to look at Jenna to see that it had purely been an accident of birth that he had so much, while she cleaned houses for a living.

"I'll give you the ball, and the photo shoot, and then we'll make the announcement, go our separate ways."

Her eyes twinkled with happiness, and she clasped her hands together. "Thank you, thank you, thank you," she cried, suddenly uplifted by his decision. She was almost about to throw her arms around his neck but he maintained a stern expression which seemed to hold her at bay. "I'll need to come here a few times in the coming weeks to prepare."

He lifted an eyebrow. "To prepare what?"

"We have to stage the house. The magazine wants to do the photo shoot two days before the ball. It will take two days with all the stylists and photographers, and a team of people to get everything ready. And for the ball, after, I'll need to get the caterers and—"

He was regretting his decision already. "How much money is this ball going to cost?"

"I'm still working that out. Pennington was going to help me. We don't have much time."

He slapped a hand to his face. It was going to be a nightmare, he could feel it in his bones already.

"It will be less than a week of interruptions, and then I will be gone," she assured him.

One week of interruptions, and then he would be free. He had no choice but to go through with it.

# CHAPTER 13

The Valentine's Day Ball and the photo shoot were still going to happen. Reed had announced it a few days ago, after Olivia had come over and both of them had disappeared into his study. It had been clear from the way they were afterwards, that they had obviously made up.

Jenna wondered how long this truce would last. From the arguments she'd heard between them, they were different people, but she could see the attraction. Reed needed a trophy wife, and Olivia needed his money and prestige. It was a perfect match made in heaven, unlike all of Jenna's past relationships with the many losers she had dated.

She cringed each time she thought about her past mistakes, and was determined not to make the same mistakes again now that she was back in Starling Bay. Her main focus was to earn a living first, and then worry about the lack of love in her life later.

The butler didn't like her, but that was fine since the feeling was mutual. She didn't care for him much either. Being poor and broke, as she had been most of her life, she was used to people looking at her, judging her, and the blue-tipped hair added to that. The way Pennington's cold eyes had looked her over, told her all she needed to know of how he saw her. And her thoughts had been confirmed by the way he'd fawned over Olivia the moment she had walked in.

Yesterday he'd given her a list of rooms to be cleaned, in order to prepare for the big events taking place within the next few weeks. Jenna didn't like taking orders, and least of all from him, but she had to do as she was asked.

She had started to make Reed's smoothie, as she did first thing after she arrived, when Pennington told her to clean the library again. "I already cleaned that last week," she told him, throwing carrots and ginger into the blender.

"That was last week," Pennington stated, calmly. "I'm telling you do to it again this week. Olivia and Reed are having a photo shoot a few days before the ball, and the library is one of the rooms Olivia says she needs."

"I'll clean it in a few days' time, otherwise it will get dusty again in time for the shoot."

"I would rather you do it now."

"And I would rather do it in a few days' time." Apparently, the butler had also booked a specialized company to come and wax the floors of the ballroom in preparation for the ball.

"And I'm telling you to—"

"I heard you, Pennington. I'm not deaf, but it seems like you're not hearing me. I will clean the library a couple of days before the shoot."

"Why can't you do as you're told?" he snapped.

"What's going on?" Reed asked, casually walking in. He seemed to gravitate towards the kitchen at around the time she would be making his light snack and smoothie.

"She's not doing as she's asked," Pennington complained.

"That's because I assume Jenna is capable of knowing what she needs to do and getting it done in a timely manner." Reed walked over to her.

"Your smoothie's almost done," she said, throwing in an apple and a cucumber. As soon as Pennington opened his mouth, she turned the blender back on again, so that the noise drowned out his voice.

"We don't have long to go, Reed. Olivia has a timetable of events and they are running like clockwork." Pennington pressed his thin, wormy lips together, and looked annoyed. "I obviously went away at the wrong time. Trust me to find everything in shambles by the time I get back."

"What do you mean everything is in shambles?" Jenna cried. "I've done what I'm supposed to do."

"And she's made me the most nutritious snacks. Thank you," Reed said, lifting the plate with his food and going over to the sit at the kitchen island.

"That's hardly her job," Pennington protested. "You need a proper chef. I'll get the agency to find one," he said, and pulled out his cell phone.

"I told you there's no need," Reed said firmly.

"Cecile could be away for weeks," Pennington protested.

"I told her to take as long as she needed to be with her sister."

"You can't live on bread rolls and sandwiches until then."

Reed threw him a peculiar look. "I'm not going to die of starvation, Pennington, and I order takeout in the evenings. I find your concern most touching, if a little over the top." He lifted his roll with both hands. "And this? This is delicious." He bit into his olive bread roll with exaggerated enthusiasm.

"Glad you like it," Jenna replied, feeling pleased. Maybe she could progress to making simple pasta dishes for him next. It would annoy Pennington no end. Yes, she decided. She would.

"I'll get a chef in. You can't survive on takeout and bread."

"This is hardly Alcatraz," Reed replied.

The butler looked none too pleased. "I'll clean the library in a few days' time," Jenna said, and walked over to Reed to hand him his smoothie.

"Thank you."

"I'm going to stick to my cleaning schedule," she announced, "And I'll get to the library when I'm good and ready."

"But Olivia said—"

"I don't care what Olivia said," Jenna interrupted. The words shot out faster than she had intended. Relenting, "I mean, there's no point in cleaning the library today, if you need it clean for the photo shoot next week."

"The photo shoot's happening in the library?" asked Reed, as if this was news to him.

"Apparently." Jenna slipped on her cleaning apron.

"I thought it was happening in the ballroom," Reed continued.

"It's taking place in different parts of the house," Pennington announced.

Reed slammed down his sandwich. "Pain in the–"

"It's going to be a great piece of publicity—" Pennington started to say.

"I don't need publicity," Reed barked. "You're beginning to sound like Olivia."

Pennington looked visibly affronted. "I have errands to run for Olivia," he muttered and started to walk away.

"For Olivia?" Reed asked.

"Yes." Pennington replied, "For the photo shoot."

"I didn't realize you were on her payroll."

"Is there a problem?" the butler asked.

"No problem."

Both she and Reed looked on as Pennington left, apparently in a mild huff.

"Say it," Reed said, picking up his half-empty glass.

She was curious, about his engagement, but could hardly ask him. It seemed to her that Reed had relented and now seemed fine with both the photoshoot and the ball going ahead. Whatever type of relationship Reed and his fiancée had, it had a touch of crazy about it. One minute they were at each other's throats and then the next they were getting ready for lovey-dovey photoshoots to show their love off to the world.

It was insane how these people lived.

But even though she couldn't say anything about what she had overheard, she had plenty to say about his butler. "You won't like it."

Reed drained his glass dry. "Say it anyway."

"Is he running this household or are you?"

"I wonder about that myself." Reed grinned, then held out his glass. "Is there any more?"

"Plenty," she said, feeling happy that he seemed to look forward to what she made each day. She refilled his glass. "I'd better get to it."

"Thanks," he took the glass. "And stick to your schedule. Don't listen to Pennington. He's not as evil as he comes across."

"I'll reserve judgment on that." She smiled at him. "It might take me a few extra hours a day, all this extra cleaning."

"Can you manage it?"

"What do you mean can I manage it? Of course I can."

"I didn't mean that. I know you can manage it. I meant what with your other jobs. I don't want you overworking to the point of exhaustion."

"You don't need to worry about me."

"I'm not." He wiped his hands on a napkin, and it seemed to her that he wanted to say something.

"Say it," she urged him.

He paused at first, then, "I found a spare bike out in one of the sheds in the yard."

She frowned, not understanding his line of conversation. Also, it could hardly be called a yard, the acres of land around the mansion were beautiful. And she didn't recall seeing a shed, unless he was referring to one of those outbuildings across the lawn.

"A bike?"

"A spare bike," he said, carefully. "I was wondering if you might like it."

"I already have a bike."

"I've seen it, but this is a spare one. It's lying around not being used, and it seems more robust than the one you have."

He'd caught her completely by surprise, and for a moment she didn't know what to say. "The one I have runs just fine."

"It's outside, next to your one, if you want to take a closer look and decide. I had it cleaned and made sure—"

"You asked Pennington to clean it?" she asked, knowing there was obviously nobody else to do it. The thought of the butler doing anything for her was hard to fathom.

But when Reed looked at her in silence, a guilty expression crossing his face, she was shocked. "*You* cleaned it?" The man who never got his hands dirty, whom she could never imagine going into the sheds to retrieve the bike, let alone make sure it was in good working order, had done all this himself?

"It wasn't that dirty."

She was speechless. And there was also the other question. *Why?*

"Come outside and take a look," he urged her again. "It's yours if you want it."

She followed him outside, feeling odd that they were doing this, and that he was giving her a spare bike.

"What do you think?" he asked, looking pleased with himself.

It looked robust, slightly old-fashioned, with its higher saddle, and smaller wheels. It was quaint, too, with a basket in front, just like in the olden days, she imagined. There was probably some truth to it, that he'd found it in the shed outside. It might even have belonged to his mother.

"You're sure this is safer than the one I have?" she asked, carefully examining the handlebars and the wheels. Everything looked new, if a little dated.

"Yes. I wouldn't have offered it otherwise. It's barely been used."

"But, *why?*"

They stared at one another. He didn't try to explain, and she didn't pursue it. He was right of course. Shay's bicycle was old, and she was sure the wheel at the back had a slow puncture which she'd been meaning to get fixed, but for now she'd managed by pumping it up before each journey.

"It's got character," she said, slowly.

"Do you like it?"

"I'm … I don't know what to say, except, thank you. It's very considerate of you to lend me this."

"Lend," he muttered, chuckling to himself. "If it makes you feel better to *borrow* it, then by all means borrow it. I'll sleep better at night knowing you're not coming to work in a deathtrap."

"I had no idea I was giving you sleepless nights."

She saw his Adam's apple move, saw him hold back from replying.

She was just about to thank him again, when he asked her, "Why didn't you tell me?"

"Tell you what?"

"Who you were."

She felt the blood drain from her face. *He knew.* "Jenna Lawson," he continued, watching her carefully. "You came to my party. We went to the same school. Why didn't you say something?"

How long had he known for? "Yeah, well," she replied,

reaching back and retying the strings on the back of her apron. "What's the big deal?"

"It is a big deal, considering you work for me and you didn't think to mention it."

She looked at him. "When did you find out?"

"A few weeks ago. My friend told me."

"Which friend?"

"Rourke Halloran. He used to be on the baseball team. He and Gail Nevis were the prom king and queen at the graduation prom."

"I wasn't here for prom."

"You weren't?"

*He didn't remember?* "I left before then."

"Right, so you did. That's what Rourke said. Why did you move?" he asked.

"My dad got a new job."

He shook his head slowly. "I never realized you'd left."

*He never realized.* He'd been solely responsible for that most humiliating episode of her teen years, and he didn't even remember that she'd left school soon after. Meanwhile, she'd carried that embarrassing moment around with her for years. She now stared at him in disbelief. "Well, I suppose that's the difference between us," she said, marching towards the house.

"What's that?" he demanded. She walked away, not even bothering to answer.

"Wait!" His raised voice halted her. Footsteps behind her told her he'd followed her. She started to walk again. "Jenna, wait. I never meant to upset you. We were messing about."

He'd opened a can of worms. "That memory," she said, turning around slowly, "that day you closed the door on me, you have no idea how that made me feel." She was holding back a decade of pent-up frustration.

"It was supposed to be a joke. I closed the door on you, because my friends made me."

"I never had you down for being spineless."

"I opened the door again, I swear I did, but my friends pushed me away."

"It was *your* party," she cried, the anger rising in her voice.

"We were boys! We were being silly. A couple of them pummeled me to the ground—"

"Some friends."

"That's what boys do!"

"You can't live behind that for the rest of your life."

"I honestly don't remember that incident much, and I don't remember you falling but Rourke said he does. He says you tripped and split your skirt, and everyone laughed."

She swallowed, going back in time to that moment, she could feel the door slam shut in her face, as hard as a slap across her cheek. She heard the laughter, cruel as a knife-blade on skin. "That event has been fixed in my mind for years. You don't know how humiliating it was. You don't know what it was like to get an invite to Reed Knight's party, to finally feel that you were worthy of the '*It*' crowd, and then to be turned away so cruelly, like you were the butt of someone's joke. It wasn't nice."

"I get that now, Jenna, but if I didn't know what happened, how could I feel bad about it?"

She stared at him defiantly. "Maybe when you didn't see me or my friends at the party? Maybe then you might have realized you'd gone too far?"

"There were over a hundred kids at that party. I didn't keep tabs on who was where."

"That's a lame answer, and you know it."

"I didn't know you fell down, Jenna, and I didn't laugh. How can I make it up to you when I wasn't the one who turned you away?"

But he hadn't recognized her either. It had taken his friend Rourke to tell him. Clearly, she'd never been on his radar. He hadn't even remembered helping her up from the track that day she fell. She'd imagined that moment as being wrapped up in some romantic notion, that he might had seen her as someone nice, someone he had noticed, as someone he might want to get to know.

But, no.

He'd barely remembered her.

She had no real answer for him, because she didn't want his pity. "You hurt me."

"I'm sorry. I can't go back in time to fix that, Jenna, but I'm here now, and I can fix things going forward."

She wanted to say more but her voice would betray her. She had never dreamed of confronting him, had never envisaged she might have the opportunity. Now that he'd brought it up, she felt a sense of peace.

He could explain it away however he wanted to, it didn't matter. That event was over, and she needed to forget about it.

"I would rather that you didn't bring this up again," she said, heading back to the house wishing she hadn't accepted his offer of the bike. It only made her feel obligated to him, and she didn't want to feel anything of the sort.

# CHAPTER 14

*H*e returned from a business meeting the following day, too late to catch Jenna, but found to his surprise that she'd made him a quick pasta dish instead of the regular sandwiches. He wondered if this was some sort of thanks for the bike.

As the days passed, Reed didn't hear any more disagreements between Pennington and Jenna, and he didn't bury himself way in the study so much either.

Some days he preferred to work in the kitchen for a few hours because not only did it afford him a beautiful view of his yard, but the brightness of the kitchen was appealing and a huge contrast to the dark, oak-paneled study.

Pennington was often busy running errands for Olivia. She had him searching for crystal cut vases and had placed orders with the florist. Whether the flowers were for the photo shoot or the ball, Reed wasn't sure, and he didn't care. He wasn't happy to sign the checks off, but he wanted a quiet life back again, and going along with this farce was his route to that paradise.

One day, as he was working away in the kitchen, the sound of rain bucketing down in sheets caught his attention. He liked this most of all; working with the sky turning dark, and the sound of heavy rain falling. The distant sound of Jenna's clanging and banging interrupted him and provided strange comfort to his ears.

Several hours later, he was still in the kitchen working when Jenna walked in. She looked weary.

"Long day?" he asked.

"Very." She slipped off her apron. "I'm done for the day. I did a few hours because that butler of yours demanded I clean two of the reception rooms again."

"He demanded?" Reed asked, "I told him that you would clean the rooms according to your schedule."

"Well, not exactly demanded. He 'suggested' that those rooms could do with a clean."

"Ah. At least he's making suggestions as opposed to ordering you about. I'd say you're training him well," he replied, barely suppressing his amusement. She and Pennington were so different. He was one of the old guard, and had been in the family for decades. He also believed that there was a hierarchy and he presided at the top. Jenna was nothing like that. If there was anything he could detect from her, she didn't give a hoot, hierarchy or not. "Is he being disrespectful to you?"

"Not more so than usual."

"I'll have a word with him."

"Please don't. I can fight my own battles."

"I'm well aware of that."

"Do you have a problem with me answering back to him?"

"No. I wouldn't dare to get in the way."

They stared at one another for a fleeting second, before she forced herself to look away. "I'd better get going."

He looked outside. It had turned dark, and it was raining heavily, and he didn't like the idea of her cycling back in this weather.

"Wait a while," he suggested. "Until the rain clears. It's pouring buckets, and you'll get soaked."

"I'll be fine. I've got a waterproof jacket." But even she looked slightly unsure.

"You must be hungry," he said, closing his laptop. "You've worked extra hours today. Why don't you have something to eat here?"

"No. No, I couldn't. It wouldn't..."

"It wouldn't what?"

It wouldn't be right. That's what she was probably thinking. He pushed back from his seat. "I have some takeout I ordered from Fellini's yesterday." He got up, and walked towards the refrigerator.

"I really shouldn't," she insisted.

"*Shouldn't* is a word you really shouldn't use."

"Easy for you to say."

"It's shrimp with linguine. It's good, and tastes great even the next day." He considered ordering takeout right now, but guessed that having her wait for food to come might put her off. He could tell she was hungry because she looked hungry, and because she wasn't arguing with him about it. It was already hours past the time she would normally be here.

"There's something I wanted to run by you," he said, emptying the contents of the take-out boxes onto a plate. His remark seemed to catch her interest.

"Like what?"

"Sit down and I'll explain." He noticed that she sat down immediately. "You okay with me microwaving it?"

She shrugged, and looked at him as if he was asking a stupid question. "Want me to do it?" she offered.

"I've got it. I can handle this. There's not much I can handle around the house, but the microwave I can."

"No wonder you need the butler."

He snorted. There was no love lost between her and Pennington.

"Isn't Olivia coming over?"

"For?" He stared at her face, trying to gauge the reason behind her question.

"Aren't you supposed to be discussing the forthcoming events? Your butler seems more concerned by them than you are."

"That's because my butler doesn't have to worry about the things that keep me awake at night."

"Thank you," she said, when he pulled out a plate and split the food between them.

"That's too much for me," she cried, when he pushed a plate towards her. "You have that," she pointed at the bigger portion.

"I already had a late lunch. That was nice, by the way, the sandwich you made today."

"I wasn't sure if you'd like beets," she replied. "Most men don't like to go too healthy."

He wondered if that reference to *most men* included her boyfriend; and whether she had a boyfriend. "It was good. Different, but good."

"*This* is really good," she said between mouthfuls, as she dug in. She was hungry. It didn't take a private investigator to come to that conclusion.

They ate in silence for a while, and then he asked her. "Would you be able to work on Saturday night, the weekend of the ball?"

Her eyes registered surprise at first, before turning angry. "You want me to clean the house while you're having the ball?"

"Not clean. *Supervise.*"

"Won't that annoy your butler?"

"He'll have plenty of other things to keep an eye out for. I would rather you keep an eye on the caterers, since you're now familiar with the house and the kitchen. Cecile still won't be back by then, and I would rather that Pennington take care of the matters at the front of the house, while you are more behind the scenes."

"Behind the scenes," she muttered. "Of course."

"I didn't mean it like that."

"No? Then how did you mean it?"

"I meant that you know where everything is in the kitchen. You have a good eye for detail, and you're organized."

"And how do you know that?"

He couldn't answer that. He just knew.

"'Cause if you're saying that to dig yourself out of that hole you just got yourself into, I'm not stupid. I know with you Knights, it's all about looking the part and—"

And she was off on another rant.

"Hey," he said, putting down his fork, and getting defensive. "That wasn't how I meant it. Pennington takes care of the security, and he's in charge of the valet boys and the guest list. He knows all the guests. He knows who's who." No sooner had he said that than he knew that she was going to take offense at that. And she did.

"Of course he would. Your butler's going to be running the show, and why wouldn't he? He likes for people to know that he's at the top, that I'm lesser, that—"

He stared at her with something bordering on mild amusement. "I like that about you."

She stopped her sentence midway.

"I've actually said something to shut you up," he said with a grin. Now he knew where her Achilles heel was.

"You like what about me?" she asked, slowly.

"I like that you don't hold back on saying what you think of people."

She opened her mouth, probably to protest, and then closed it again. It surprised him, because she was completely speechless now. "I don't think..." she cleared her throat. "I don't think your butler would be too pleased if he saw me sitting here eating with you."

"I don't care what he thinks."

"Your fiancée wouldn't be too pleased either."

"She doesn't live here," he said, expertly twirling the linguine around his fork. "But I expect you already gathered that."

"I had noticed she wasn't here much."

"She was in the beginning, but she'd bring her friends over every other weekend, and suddenly there would be four of five women here, and they'd stay not for a weekend, but for a long weekend. This place is huge, and there's a whole other wing to it that's barely used, but she would be here, at this end, because the rooms are used, and are more opulent, I suppose. Anyway, with all that noise, I couldn't concentrate. So I bought her a condo in Forest Heights."

Jenna almost choked on her pasta. She thought of the sofa where she slept, with its frayed edges on the cushions, and how she had fallen off it when she'd turned. She couldn't afford to rent a place for herself, and Reed had bought his fiancée a condo so that she could hang out there with her friends and not disturb him. For a moment she forgot to eat.

"What's wrong?" he asked. She'd lifted her fork and was staring at him speechless. "Has it gone cold?"

"No, it's fine. It's…it's good." She ate, and waited, then, "So you decided to buy her the condo, to get some space?"

He didn't answer straightaway. "You could say that. Hmm, to get some space," he murmured to himself. "Maybe I did."

"I'll try and be more quiet when I'm cleaning."

"*More* quiet?" He burst out laughing. "Were you ever trying to be?"

"Yes! Why?" She looked surprised. "Am I not quiet?"

"Hardly."

She gasped. "You should have said that I was disturbing you."

"You're not as loud as Olivia."

She opened her mouth to say something, but he said it instead. "You can take that as a compliment."

She nodded.

"She's not too fond of this old house, either," he explained, "That was the other reason she preferred the condo. Olivia finds this stuffy, and depressing, and old." There were other reasons but none that Jenna needed to know.

"She doesn't like this house?"

He caught the surprise in her voice. "But it's beautiful, all those high ceilings, and stained glass windows, and the architecture."

"Thank you. Olivia doesn't care for it much." He sat back and absorbed her words. He loved the house too. He had fleetingly considered selling it, or renting it out and moving to something smaller, more practical, but his father had forbidden him to, telling him that the Knight mansion was almost like a landmark, sitting on the extreme corner of Starling Bay. Besides, he had grown up in this house, and had many happy memories, as did his parents, except that they now chose to live out in Montana, and spend their days in nature. Still, they loved having this home to come back to whenever they wanted. In his future, the one with children, and a wife, Reed imagined making more happy memories.

"I hated it before, but now that I've been here, I've come to see how truly stunning it is," Jenna told him. "I've never been in something so grand before."

"I don't suppose the other houses you cleaned took up so much time?"

"Other houses?"

"At your interview, you said you'd cleaned other houses." He was toying with her.

"I think we both know that I only cleaned my room and it

wasn't big. The entire shared apartment was probably the size of one of your reception rooms."

He winced, unable to comprehend what that must have been like. "I'm sorry," he replied, because he didn't know what else to say.

"I'm not. Like most things in my life, it was a learning experience. Just because you don't have the good things in life doesn't mean you can't appreciate beauty when you see it."

He held her gaze and caught a glimpse of something, hesitation, or unease, for she chewed her lip.

"My company has just won the project to carry out the refurbishment on the old movie theater."

"You mean that old building near Fellini's?"

"That's the one."

"When did that close?" she asked.

"When we were still at school. Maybe thirteen, fourteen years ago. We're going to re-open it once we've renovated it."

She nodded approvingly. "It's a beautiful building."

"That's what I thought. We're keeping all the old features." He made a mental note to show it to her when they had the opening night. "I'm sorry you've had such bad memories of this place," he said, keen to help her shed them.

"Don't be," she replied quickly, then started eating again.

He didn't want to make her feel uncomfortable again. "I'm glad you like that" he said, changing the subject. "The pasta, I mean."

"It's lovely. So much better than the pasta I made for you the other day."

"That was good, too."

But why, he wondered? Why had she gone the extra mile to make him sandwich rolls and now pasta, when he hadn't even asked for it. He didn't pursue the matter, and was grateful anyway.

He couldn't remember the last time he had sat here and eaten dinner with Olivia. All of a sudden he felt uncomfortable that he'd made a mental comparison of Jenna and Olivia in his head. It didn't seem right, but at the same time, the conversation had left him feeling warm, and happy inside, and wanting to know more. And that didn't feel right, either.

Jenna's clean plate was evidence enough of how much she had enjoyed the food, and he was glad he'd asked her to stay and eat. "So, on Saturday night. Can you work? I'll pay double-time on account of it being a weekend night."

"Yes. I can work. How many hours do you need me for?"

"As many as you want to do. The party starts at 7:00 p.m., maybe you could come a few hours before. I'm sure they'll be setting up for it from 4:00 p.m. onwards, and then it goes on until the early hours of the morning. So as many hours as you want, at double the pay."

He could see her doing mental calculations. "I'll be here at 4:00 p.m."

"Great." There was one other matter to take care of. He walked towards her and pulled out a bunch of twenty dollar bills. "I think that might cover it, but it would be better if you—"

She didn't take the money. "What's this for?" She looked embarrassed. "You don't pay me directly. The agency does that."

"A dress," he replied, suddenly feeling embarrassed. He avoided looking at her. "It might be better if you didn't wear a cleaning apron that night. A black dress will be fine."

"I already have a dress."

"Something plain and simple." *But elegant*, he wanted to add, but he knew that would set her off. It was funny, and refreshing, that he was filtering what he was saying on account of upsetting her.

"I'll wear the one I have." She stared at him full of defiance.

"It's got a thigh-high slit, and it's a halter neck. Will that be a problem?"

The thought of her wearing *that* outfit did something to him. He couldn't find a suitable reply. "And…and you'll have to put your hair up."

"Is this a party or a funeral?"

*A thigh-high slit and a halter neck.* Her words were still ringing in his head.

She laughed. "You should see your face. You look disturbed." She snorted. "Don't worry. I can do simple and plain, and I promise not to look like a hooker."

"Take the money, please," he insisted. "You'll need it for the cab. Get a cab here, and we'll call you one at the end of the party because it will be late."

She looked at the bills as if they were dirt. "Jenna, don't make this what it isn't," he insisted.

"What am I making it about?"

"About you being a maid, and me being the rich mansion owner telling you what to wear."

"But isn't that exactly what you've just implied?"

"This isn't about me turning you away from the party back then."

"I never said it was, and I asked you never to bring that up again."

He blew out an exasperated cry. "This isn't about any divide, for goodness sake. I wouldn't let Pennington be at my party in jeans and sneakers."

"He'd look awful in jeans and sneakers."

They both burst out laughing, and then they heard the noise at the same time. It was the familiar and annoying sound of heels on wood. And then they heard Pennington's voice. Reed shoved his wallet back into his pocket, and the loose bills into the other pocket. He didn't have time to think about why he hadn't handed them over to Jenna.

A moment later Olivia and Pennington walked in.

"Hmmmm," Pennington cast his eye over the kitchen island, at the plates, at him, and then Jenna. Reed thought he saw the man's nostrils flare a little.

"This looks *cozy*," his manservant muttered. Jenna looked as if she wanted to disappear out of the window.

"I could say the same about you two," Reed remarked.

"Olivia wanted to visit the florist," Pennington explained.

"Oh? I thought the magazine people were staging the house."

"I still need flowers around the house for the ball. The magazine people aren't paying for the ball, are they?" Olivia eyed their dinner plates with suspicion. "I didn't know Jenna was having her meals here."

"I asked her to."

His ex-fiancée and butler looked at him as if he'd made a double entendre.

"I should go," said Jenna, getting up from her chair. "It's only raining a little bit now." She reached forward for his plate, but he shook his head. Instead, she took her plate to the sink, rinsed it and put it into the dishwasher.

"You've eaten," said Olivia. "I could have made something for you."

The farce, the farce, the farce. When had she ever made anything for him before? "I can't remember the last time you did that," he replied tightly, then looked out and saw that the rain had stopped. But it was dark now, and he didn't like the idea of Jenna cycling all the way back to wherever it was she lived.

The Knight mansion was away from the bay, and it was a fair distance from the town center. He had no idea where Jenna lived, but he didn't think it was anywhere near here. He could drive her home but he sensed the idea wouldn't go down well with Olivia or his butler.

"I can get Pennington to drop you off," he offered, but the I'd-rather-die look on her face told him it wasn't a good idea.

"I'll be fine."

"How do I look?" Jenna asked Shay. She had gone shopping one morning and had managed to find a black dress that was discounted because the seam holding the zipper in place had started to come undone. She had sewn it back on and the dress was as perfect as ever.

It was slim-fitting. Maybe a little *too* slim-fitting. After all she was working at the party, overseeing it, not as a guest but as an employee. She'd seen another dress that flared out from the waist downwards, but it was too long, and too sack-like. The one she had ended up buying was sleek, and practical, and...well, *sexy*.

"You look hot!" Shay exclaimed, approvingly.

"Is it *too* sexy?" Now she was worried that it might be too much.

"You can never be too sexy," replied Shay, pushing up her glasses.

"You can if you work in the Knight mansion, and I'm supposed to be working, not mingling."

"You'll fit right in."

"I don't think so."

"Jenna, stop that. Looking the way you do, you fit right in. I wonder what his fiancée's going to wear."

Whatever it was, it was going to be designer wear. Privately, Jenna wondered how Reed and Olivia would be around one another, and she was looking forward to the photo shoot the day before. It would give her plenty of time to people-watch. She'd already heard Olivia and Reed having another disagreement earlier today. Olivia seemed adamant that the photo shoot would be with both of them, and Reed seemed determined not to have any part of it.

It confused her further.

Were they together or not?

Or was this the nature of their relationship—hot and cold? It was no way to start a life together.

"She has rooms full of clothes at the mansion," Jenna told Shay. "You know how most people have closets? Olivia has *rooms*."

"I bet she has the most gorgeous clothes, and matching shoes *and* bags."

"I've no idea. I've never looked inside the closets."

"Not even peeked inside?"

"No! I would never. I'm a maid, not a snoop."

"That's some serious restraint. I'm impressed. I'd have had a good peek if I were in your shoes."

"Just be grateful you're not. I'm not sure being a maid is at the top of anyone's life wish list." She didn't intend to be a maid, or clean offices and the preschool forever. She had been looking at online book-keeping courses, and had been thinking about some sort of accreditation so that she could hopefully get some type of office job a few months down the line.

"She must go crazy with his credit cards," said Shay, sounding as if she was obsessed by Olivia's lifestyle.

"You have no idea. Reed's fed up with it all, poor man."

Shay glanced at her.

"What?" asked Jenna.

"*Poor man*? Since when did you start feeling sorry for Reed Knight?"

"Ever since he apologized for pulling that stunt at the party."

"Ever since he leant you that bike, more like," Shay offered. "I never thought I would live to witness you two getting along and you feeling sorry for him."

"I never thought I'd live to see the day when I'd be cleaning his house," complained Jenna.

"Come to think of it, you haven't said a single nasty thing about him lately."

"I didn't want to bore you."

"It's never boring hearing you lambast Reed Knight."

"He's not so bad."

"You're softening in your old age," Shay observed.

"He pays my wages."

"*One* set of them."

"True," Jenna agreed. "I'm getting double pay for the ball."

"At least one of us gets to go."

"Did you want to go?" Jenna asked.

"Anyone who's anyone in Starling Bay will be there."

"We're not anyone," Jenna reminded her. But she was going to get a peek into the party of the year, of this year at least, since Shay had told her that Reed and Olivia had hosted a New Year's Eve party a few weeks before Jenna had started working there.

She could see that Olivia was the more social of the two. Reed didn't seem happy about any of this and even the preparations for the shoot got him worked up. She couldn't tell what was going on. Even a few nights ago, when Reed had been about to give her money toward the dress, he'd put his wallet away as soon as Olivia and Pennington had turned up.

His actions had been those of a guilty man, but he hadn't done anything for which he needed to feel guilty about. Yet the expressions on both Olivia and Pennington's faces had even made her feel a little guilty.

Had she done something wrong by having dinner with Reed Knight?

It didn't matter what was going on between Reed and Olivia; it was none of her business. She was going as a maid to the party at the mansion, not as a guest, and it would be in her best interest if she remembered that.

"It's not *on* Valentine's Day, it's on the weekend, a few days after," Reed assured Rourke. "I made sure the date wouldn't clash just so that you would be available and could attend." Reed winked at Dylan conspiratorially.

"Somehow, I don't think you had much to do with it. You didn't even want to have the ball," Rourke retorted. "And what makes you think I'll be busy on Valentine's Day? I'm currently a single man."

"And I'm a Russian agent," said Dylan.

"You two have the wrong opinion of me."

"Your behavior has given us this opinion of you," Reed clarified.

"You're in a good mood today," Dylan observed.

"Why wouldn't I be?"

His friend gave him a do-you-really-want-me-to-answer-that look.

"Are there any interesting women attending, from the fashion magazine?" Rourke asked, "As in, any make-up artists?"

"They're not invited to the ball. Hopefully they'll have disappeared the day before, as soon as the photo shoot is over. At least, I hope they will." It was killing him, the thought of the upcoming week. He wasn't going to be able to get much work done.

"Why?" Dylan asked, "How many of them were you expecting to get better acquainted with?"

Rourke looked exasperated. "I date one woman at a time, but when I'm fishing, I like to cast a wide net."

"I'm loving the analogy," muttered Reed.

"So, are there?"

"Are there what?"

"Going to be any make-up artists or any such people from the fashion magazine at your house? I mean, say if I turned up at your place unexpectedly during the photo shoot?"

"To fish?" asked Dylan.

"I'm not asking *you* for advice," Rourke replied. "You're off the market, and you don't know the stress of finding someone compatible."

"Someone *compatible?*" asked Dylan, "For you?"

"Yes, me," Rourke protested. "Why do I get the feeling you two are ganging up on me now that neither of you are single?"

"Nobody's ganging up on you. Why don't you stop worrying about it, and take a break from always being on the lookout?" Dylan suggested.

"I can't help it. I'm drawn to women, it's like an incurable disease."

"My heart's bleeding for you," said Reed. "What did Merry think of the houses?" he asked, turning to Dylan.

"Merry's looking for a house?" asked Rourke.

"She was looking around Forest Heights," Dylan explained. "She likes a few of them, and it would be ideal for Spart."

"Spart?"

"Her dog," Reed replied, since Rourke clearly wasn't keeping up with things.

"What about her kid?"

"Chloe likes it here. She's the one who got her mom thinking about moving here."

"I'm sure her mom had her own reasons for wanting to move here," Reed remarked with a grin.

Rourke waded in. "For a guy who had sworn off women, it sure sucks that you've now met your perfect match. You'll be telling us you're getting married next."

"No marriage plans yet," Dylan replied smoothly, taking a sudden interest in his drink.

"*Yet?*" asked Reed, seeing his friend's face suddenly brighten. "Which seems to imply that it's in the pipeline." Dylan looked at him but said nothing.

"Speaking of marriage plans, have you two decided where you're going for the honeymoon?" Rourke asked.

Reed paused. It was on the tip of his tongue, to tell them the truth. He *wanted* to tell them, even though he hadn't come here tonight with that specific end in mind. Now that they were all together, he was desperate to let this huge weight off his chest. And yet, he could see the other problem; if he told them, they would know at the ball, and he didn't want to ruin that night for them.

He felt weak pandering to Olivia's needs—putting her selfish reasons first, instead of doing the right thing, and the right thing would have been to cancel everything, the ball, the photo shoot, and the wedding, and announce their break-up. Instead he'd opted to go along with Olivia's plan.

He had to see it through, and then he would tell them. "Not yet," he said, "Let me get this blasted photo shoot out of the way first, and that damn ball, and then we'll see."

"If you're so unhappy about the ball, why don't you tell Olivia? Why are you going through with something you don't want to do?" Dylan asked, eerily accurate once again. It made

Reed wonder if the two of them weren't psychically connected sometimes.

"Don't encourage him." Rourke piped in. "I want him to have the ball. Who doesn't want a great big party? Olivia's my kind of woman, figuratively speaking," he added quickly.

"Yeah, yeah." Reed rolled his eyes at the comment, knowing that Olivia most definitely *wasn't* Rourke's type of woman. Rourke was all bold and brash on the outside, but inside, he was different. He didn't let many people see the real him. Reed knew, though.

"As for the photo shoot, come on," Rourke placed an arm around Reed's shoulder. "It can't be all that bad. After all, who wouldn't want to be featured as a loving, gorgeous couple in next month's magazine?"

Reed plastered a smile on his face in response. The idea of the photo shoot had so angered him that he hadn't thought it through properly. He'd been thinking that it would be for Olivia's benefit, that she would waltz through the vast mansion, shedding outfits like dead skin, and the end result would be glossy photos of her in a beautiful big home, with a huge bunch of exotic flowers in the background. He hadn't thought it would involve him. That she would expect him to be in the pictures, living out the lie under the glare of the camera.

"I told Jenna," he said, suddenly remembering.

"Your maid?" asked Dylan.

"Told Jenna what?" asked Rourke.

"That I knew who she was."

"And what did she say?" Rourke asked.

"She didn't say much," he recalled. Seemed to him that she didn't really want to talk about it.

"Did it make things awkward after, with her working for you?" Dylan asked.

He had to think about it. It had made things slightly awkward, but he couldn't pinpoint whether it was because of that conversation.

"Not much." He felt different around Jenna now, that much was true, and he wasn't sure why. Maybe it was the connection from their high school days that was the cause of the shift in how they were with one another? He couldn't say for sure, but he wasn't about to tell his friends any of this.

"I'll come by your place for the photo shoot," said Rourke, inviting himself, which didn't surprise Reed. "I'm curious to see if Jenna Lawson will remember me."

"Why would she remember you?" Reed asked mildly.

"Why would she not?" Rourke gave his usual grin, and this time it irritated the heck out of him.

# CHAPTER 17

*H*e didn't look happy. Jenna could see by that scowl on Reed's face.

She had come early today, missing out on her afternoon nap and lunch. Pennington had told her there was much to be done, but with a professional cleaning company who had come in to polish the glass and silverware, and others waxing the floor of the ballroom, she didn't see that there was much else for her to do, other than to get in the way.

The Knight mansion was overrun with people. A group of people took up residence in one of the main reception rooms, and Olivia strutted around, done up in make-up and wearing a beautiful dress.

Jenna felt like an extra on a film set and, not wanting to get in the way, had gone directly upstairs to clean the bathrooms and polish the mirrors. She also wanted to steer clear of the butler, but when she had finished everything, she ventured back downstairs and contemplated fixing Reed's snacks. But as she headed towards the kitchen she could see that it was full of people. She wanted to remain invisible and out of the way. So, when she saw the stylists and photographers setting up in one of the reception rooms, she dove into the library with her duster and polish spray can.

The sweet sound of silence welcomed her as she closed the door behind her, and let out a breath. Shutting out that noise was liberating. She put down her duster and polish, and walked over to the fire which had been lit; she'd overheard Pennington say that they were going to use this room later on today for another shoot.

For now she took advantage of the silence, and sat on the cold, hard leather sofa, facing the fire and taking a much-needed break.

The door suddenly burst open, and Reed's voice thundered in, shattering the quietness. "This isn't what I signed up for."

Jenna dove onto the floor, and wriggled behind the sofa.

"But you said I could have this," Olivia whined.

The door slammed shut. It was a hard, loud slam that made her breath hitch. Jenna prayed that they wouldn't see her. She lay on the floor like a wounded dog, using the cover of the sofa to hide her. This position wasn't going to conceal her for long; Reed or Olivia only had to walk towards the fireplace, and she was toast.

"Damn it, Olivia. You said it was a photo shoot. I didn't think it would have me in it."

"We're supposed to be engaged. Why would you *not* be in it?"

"Because we are not engaged. That was part of the deal. Remember?"

"They won't give me the photo shoot if it's only me, Reed. It's because of you that I have this deal at all. It's supposed to be a society piece, on me and how the beauty queen—"

"Ex," he muttered. "You're an *ex*-beauty queen."

"Must you remind me? Must you be so cruel?"

"It's a fact, sweetheart. You'd do well to remember that."

"You're being vicious."

"*I'm* being vicious?" Jenna heard him mutter. Then, "I'm not doing it, Oliva. I have work to do, and businesses to run, and I haven't been able to concentrate because of this circus!"

Jenna's heart began to thump. Reed's voice was coming from different parts of the room. He was pacing around.

"Why don't you ask your boyfriend to pose for you, that would be more fitting, wouldn't it?" A dangerous tone laced Reed's voice.

"He's not my boyfriend. How many times do I have to tell you that? I'm loyal to you. I love you."

Jenna froze. *Boyfriend? What boyfriend?*

"Stop." Reed's ice-cold voice cut across the air. Jenna prayed that he wouldn't come closer, because he was going to be *really* mad if he caught her eavesdropping on the floor like this, looking completely ridiculous no less.

"If you're not in any of the photos, it negates the whole point of the photo shoot. Please, Reed. I'll stick to my promise. This could be a launching pad for my career—"

"Olivia!"

Pennington's voice sailed over from outside, followed by a knock.

"Wait," thundered Reed.

"Please," Olivia begged. "One photo. Just one photo, Reed."

"You realize this will all backfire, don't you? That by the time this goes to print, we will have announced our breakup?"

"Let it go to print. I'll be back in New York by then."

"You're using them, just like you use everyone around you."

"I never used you. I love you, I still do. You're the one who—"

"Enough. I don't want to hear any of this."

"One photo? Please. Just let them take one photo of you?"

So it was true? It was just as she had heard the last time. Their engagement was off. Jenna didn't dare to breathe. She lay on her belly, propped up on her elbows, with her head angled so that she could hear clearly. But her heart was beating crazily.

"I'll agree to appear in one photo only," said Reed, reluctantly. "But I am not answering any questions, I'm not taking part in any interviews, and I'm not telling any lies."

"Olivia! They're calling you." It was Pennington's voice again.

"Thank you." Olivia sounded relieved, and then Jenna heard the door open and then close.

She got onto all fours, and waited, straining her ears in case there was any indication of sound. She didn't dare to peek her head above the sofa just yet, but in the next moment she found herself instead peering at two finely polished shoes.

She almost choked with shock. Not only had she been caught, but she probably looked ridiculous on all fours. She stared up at Reed's fine features while her heart felt as if it was suffering a cardiac arrest.

"You," he said casually, with his hands in his pockets. He looked smart in his white shirt, and gray-checked slacks. She closed her eyes briefly, as if it would block out the humiliation she felt. Her brain went into overdrive as she sought a way to explain herself out of this one. "I was...taking a... break," she explained, slowly raising herself to standing. "I'm sorry, I know this looks bad but I can explain."

"What in the devil do you think you're doing?"

"I...I was just taking a break and..." That didn't come out too well. It made her sound as if she'd been slacking off. And on top of that she'd overheard the most private of conversations. This was no laughing matter, and Reed's hard face confirmed that. She stepped back, her pulse racing as the room began to spin. She couldn't think.

"You must have heard everything."

She nodded, guilt shaming her. "I'm sorry. I wanted to escape. There are people all over the place, and I'd just finished cleaning all your bathrooms and was about to go into the—"

"Stop, Jenna. Stop." His tone wasn't sharp and hard, the way it had been when he'd spoken to Olivia.

"Are you going to fire me?"

"For what?"

"For taking a break."

He chortled, and then stopped, his eyes wide with surprise. "You think I'd fire you for taking a much-needed break?"

"And for listening…it was a mistake, I swear. I didn't mean—"

"No," he replied, interrupting her. "I'm not going to fire you."

"But Pennington—" He'd fired the other maid for stealing. She was sure he'd lump Jenna's misdemeanors under the same umbrella.

"Screw Pennington," Reed replied calmly. "He's my butler, not the lord of the manor."

She relaxed her shoulders. "I shouldn't have been here, and I'm sorry I heard your conversation."

"Don't be."

"You're not mad?" Because he ought to have been. "Why aren't you mad?" she asked, out of curiosity. Maybe he was overcompensating, first with the bike, and now this.

Or was he?

Her heartrate picked up a little, just as it had started to slow down. Maybe Reed was being nice to her because he was a nice person, and because … She tried not to dwell on it, the slight, subtle, crazy little flutterings in her belly.

"It's a relief to tell someone," he replied, walking away and looking down at the fire. Unable to help herself, she stared at his back, and then his pert, tight bottom. She chewed her lower lip, as her gaze settled on his fine body for a long and guilty moment.

With effort, she forced herself to look away. She'd only had confirmation of the broken engagement a few moments ago, and yet her body was reacting as if it was having its own Macy's Christmas Day Parade. "A relief?" she asked, her voice sounding wobbly and strange.

"I've been holding it in. Haven't even told my friends or my family how bad things have become between us."

She didn't know what to say. Something rose up inside her, a flame burning brighter and stronger, mushrooming from a flicker.

"I'm not even sure what I feel for Olivia anymore."

"You don't?" Why was he telling her this? She breathed in and out, three maybe four times in the silence that followed. Reed's words were like a salve, and even though it was wrong, wrong, wrong, she felt uplifted by them. She tried to think of something to say, something to comfort him with because it was clear to her that this man was conflicted.

He wasn't a single man, she reminded herself, as far as the world was concerned, he was very much engaged. And maybe Olivia wasn't all bad. Maybe they were both going through a hard time, what with the pressures of Reed's businesses, and Olivia's stresses from the photoshoot and the ball.

Reed was quiet as he continued to stare into the fire.

"You're both probably having pre-wedding jitters," she said, trying to be helpful, trying to find a way to soothe him, trying to suppress the sudden, unexpected surge of hope floating inside her.

"You get pre-wedding jitters a day or two before the wedding," he replied. "Not four months before." He turned around and stared at her, his gaze spearing her heart in a way that kept her pinned where she was. She couldn't talk, or move, or respond.

This was wrong. Very wrong, she told herself.

"What were you doing on the floor?" he asked.

"I dropped to the floor when I heard your voice, and I couldn't get up. I was too scared to."

"Too scared to? *You?*" he asked, sounding doubtful. His lips turned up at the corners in a hint of a smile. "I can't imagine you being afraid of anything."

"Olivia hates me, and I was worried that she might fire me on the spot if I got up."

"She can't fire you, because you work for me. Only I have that privilege."

Her nostrils would have flared at that, but she forced herself to let him have it. "I won't tell a soul, I promise. I'll keep it all to myself," she told him.

"You might be doing me a favor if you did tell, at least then people would know."

"I'm not the type to go around spreading rumors."

"I'm sure you've heard of things by now that you've probably told your roommate."

"I haven't told her a thing."

"No?" he raised an eyebrow.

"No. I don't see the point in spreading people's misery."

He lifted his head, eyed her for a few moments.

"Why are you going along with something you don't want?" she asked.

"The engagement, you mean?"

"That, and the photoshoot. I thought it was only people like me who did things they didn't want to do."

"We all have things we would rather not do, Jenna. That's a universal decree. Having money doesn't preclude people from that. I'm going along with this nonsense because I figure I owe her this much at least."

She bit her lower lip, and he stared at it; his focus on that made her chew it some more.

"You're nervous," he noted.

She tilted her chin up and stared at his face, then wondered if Reed Knight had always looked this handsome. "I'm…" What could she say? "I feel silly that you caught me in an act."

"In an *act*?" he laughed. "That has almost sexual undertones to it."

That made her blush. "I didn't mean like that." She stared at her hands, unable to look at him.

Something invisible, and shapeless, and formless had passed between them just now. It was a feeling that she couldn't name, or pinpoint, or describe.

"I forgot to give you money for the dress," he said, pulling out his wallet, and taking out some bills. His blue eyes searched hers, then widened for the tiniest of seconds. "Take it," he said, when she hesitated.

"Reed!" It was Pennington's voice at the door again.

"Not now—" Reed roared, but it was too late. Pennington walked in, and his mouth fell open at the sight of Reed holding out money for her.

"I didn't know you were …busy," the butler said, a veil of suspicion settling on his face.

"I told you not now," Reed snapped. He closed his palm with the bills in it. That very movement must have looked suspect, Jenna thought. She didn't want to know what the silver-haired, straight-laced enemy standing at the door might have thought of it.

"Very well." Pennington stepped back, and backed out of the door, like a robot.

"He's going to have the knives out for me," Jenna murmured.

"Don't worry about him."

"Easy enough for you to say." She imagined running into the man at the top of the stairs and him pushing her down them. Her imagination often went to cinematic places in the heat of a moment.

"Jenna," Reed's voice was gentle, and the softness of it made her turn her head towards him. "Don't worry about him. Here," he held the bills towards her again.

"That didn't…" she started to say. "That didn't look right." She tried to reassure herself. There was nothing untoward in their conversation, in their being here like this, was there? "We didn't do anything," she blurted out loud. The heat of Reed's stare made her want to curl up and die. He was probably wondering if she'd lost her brains down the toilet when she had been cleaning it earlier.

"Do anything? Like what?" he asked, making her tremble at the connotations behind that question. Right now she wished her head was plated with industrial strength steel, so that this man couldn't reach inside and know what she had been thinking. And when she couldn't find her voice, nor move her lips to formulate a reply, he asked, "You're worried that he saw me giving you money?"

"Yes." Could he not see that? The two of them here, in the library, talking in secret like this. It most definitely looked suspicious. "I can buy myself a dress," she replied, ignoring the twisting sensation in her stomach. Composing herself with every ounce of willpower, she told him, "I'm not living below the poverty line." *Almost*, but not quite.

"Okay, fine. I didn't want to put you out of pocket, that's all. And get a cab here and back on the day. Take the money out of the jar if you don't want to take it from me." He slipped the money back into his wallet.

"For the cab I will."

"How's the bike?"

"Great. No punctures."

"That's a bonus."

"Pretty big bonus, if you ask me." She smiled. "I need to finish the cleaning." She was eager to leave, but not so eager to run into Pennington. He would have told Olivia, and she didn't relish the thought of both him and Olivia ganging up on her.

# CHAPTER 18

The madness continued to the next day. The only reason he was able to get through it was knowing that today, the whole team of sycophants would pack up their bags and go.

There was only one more day of insanity let, and it would be over after the ball tomorrow.

"That was perfect, Mr. Knight. Are you sure we can't get you to pose over by the fireplace with your fiancée?"

Over my dead body, he thought, as he wiped the gunk they had put on his face. 'Light make-up,' they told him, 'you'll look natural. You won't even notice you have anything on.' "I'm sure," he replied, firmly. "How much longer?" He waved his moist cloth at the scene in front of him, desperate for them to leave.

"Just a couple more hours, sir."

A couple more hours, he thought. He was going to take his laptop over to the other wing of the house and disappear for a few hours, but as he neared his study, he saw Rourke talking to Jenna in the kitchen.

"Well, look at you!" Rourke hollered as soon as he saw him. Jenna turned her head away. He felt as if she had been avoiding him, for some reason. He usually caught sight of her, even with the circus show taking place around him, but today he had barely seen her. "Hi," he said to both of them. "I see you've met."

"Can't miss the blue hair," Rourke replied.

"Is he bothering you?" Reed asked Jenna, examining her face. She shook her head.

"He's being very nice, which is surprising given that both of you were part of a group of guys that my friends and I hated back at school."

"*That* was a misunderstanding," said Rourke. "That time at the party."

"I've already explained," Reed stepped in, but he also knew this wasn't a conversation that Jenna would want to have.

"I like her blue hair."

Reed nodded. "It grows on you, after a while."

Jenna wasn't joining in. She had her hands in the front pocket of her cleaning apron, and looked as if she couldn't wait to get away.

"Is that makeup?" Rourke asked him, making a face.

"For the cameras." He wiped the cloth over his face again, and stared at the gunk that came off. "Light makeup, my butt," he muttered. "How do you women get through the day wearing this muck?" he asked Jenna.

"I don't wear much makeup."

"You don't need it," he said, without thinking.

She seemed shocked by his reply.

"So, tell me how it's been," said Rourke, plugging the obvious gap in conversation.

"A complete waste of my time," Reed moaned. "Do you have any idea how disruptive this has been?"

"Then why did you agree to go along with it?" Rourke asked, jokingly.

"I should go and clean something," said Jenna, suddenly. "Before Pennington finds me doing nothing."

"Is he giving you a hard time?" Reed was worried knowing what his butler could be like.

"No," Jenna replied. She seemed eager to leave, and he didn't know why.

"It was nice talking to you," Rourke told her. "I'll catch up with you tomorrow." Jenna smiled and walked away. "She'll be here tomorrow, won't she?"

"To work," Reed clarified. Why the heck did Rourke seem so keen for her to be here?

"To work, yeah, that's what I meant. You're not supposed to be paying compliments to the maid."

Reed's mouth tightened. "Why? Because she's a maid?" He hadn't been paying Jenna a compliment, he'd been telling the truth.

"Because you're engaged."

"And I can't tell the truth?"

"Not when you're talking about your maid."

"What does her being a maid have to do with anything?" He was curious to know what Rourke had a problem with the most; the fact that he'd complimented a woman who wasn't his fiancée, or the fact that she was a maid, or both.

"Because you're engaged. I'm the one who does stuff like that, not you."

"I only said she didn't need make-up. I didn't make a move on her."

"You can't," Rourke remarked. "You're getting married in four months."

Reed stopped himself from saying something. His friends were going to have a huge shock when he announced that the engagement was off. It was going to be the stuff of nightmares and he wasn't looking forward it.

"Dylan's worried about you, you know that?" Rourke said.

"Is he?" That surprised him. He had obviously been worried about it enough to mention it to Rourke. "He doesn't need to be."

"He is, because that's what we do, we look out for each other."

"It's business pressure."

"That's what I told him."

"And?"

"And he agreed."

Rourke scanned around the room. "Are you going to show me around and introduce me to the team?"

"Oh, yes, I forgot. You came to check out the hot women on the set." How could he forget? This had been the sole purpose of his friend's visit. "You don't need me to show you around. Why don't you just wander around at your leisure, and take all the time you need?"

He had work to do.

He disappeared into his study to get his laptop and files together, so that he could go to the study at the other end of the house. The door was open, but Pennington knocked, and waited. "Yes," said Reed, looking up.

"Will you need lunch?"

"Jenna always makes lunch."

"She said she's not feeling well, and she's going home early."

Going home early? He wondered if she would be well enough to come tomorrow.

"Lunch?" Pennington asked again.

"I'll get something later," he replied. He would go out once he'd dealt with some of the urgent matters that had been piling up. Pennington lingered near the door. "I was wondering if we should use this time to think about getting a qualified cleaner in."

Reed put down his laptop. "A qualified cleaner?" he asked. "You mean, one who has a college degree in the art of cleaning?"

Pennington's thin lips suppressed a smile. "Jenna doesn't have the required cleaning experience."

"And how would you know that?"

"I called the agency and asked to see her resume."

"You did what?" He hadn't seen a copy of Jenna's resume himself. The lady at the recruitment agency had called him and sent Jenna over the same day and he'd hired her without needing to see any paperwork. He didn't like this sneakiness from Pennington. "What were you doing going behind my back and calling the agency?" he thundered. "Are you deliberately looking to find dirt on Jenna?"

"I was looking out for you, the way I always do. Every person coming to work here has to be carefully vetted. You can never be too sure."

"Jenna's doing a fantastic job," Reed stated. "I don't understand why you find fault with every maid I take on."

"The last one stole from you," Pennington reminded him.

"Jenna hasn't stolen from me or done anything wrong."

"I feel responsible, since I wasn't here to overlook this hire. I apologize if I've offended you in any way." Pennington walked backwards, and closed the door.

Reed wondered what this was about, but he wasn't sure if people were making something out of nothing, or if it was his guilty conscience making him think this way.

# CHAPTER 19

Shay wolf-whistled.

"Stop it!" Jenna cried, smoothing down the dress. She turned to her side and looked at her full-length reflection in the mirror. She looked good. Now she worried that the dress might be a little too tight. She didn't want to send out the wrong message. She wondered what Pennington would make of it. As it was, the butler had his claws out for her, and so did Olivia.

"Is it too tight?" She looked at Shay's face.

"It is *beautifully* tight. Not *can't-sit-in-this* tight, but *sending-out-a-signal-to-the-world* tight."

Jenna screwed up her face. That wasn't the reaction she was after. "I don't want to send out a signal to *anyone*."

"That's not what I meant," said Shay, getting up from the sofa and walking over. Standing behind her, she placed her hands on Jenna's shoulders and forced her to look in the mirror. "You look elegant. *Classy,* is the word I would use, and this twist suits you." She wolf-whistled again.

"Will you stop doing that?" Jenna begged. Okay, she had to admit, she *did* look good, she looked better than she had in months, and with her hair up in a sleek knot, thanks to Shay's help, she had cleaned up well. Now she worried that it might be too much. That she looked as if she'd made a huge effort getting dressed for tonight. She wondered what Reed would think.

Why did it matter what he thought? It shouldn't have, but it did. Now all of a sudden she was worried about how he might interpret her appearance, and her survival instincts had kicked in—the ones that had helped her fend off over-eager customers when she'd been waitressing back in Chicago. She had seen that look on Pennington's face when he'd walked in on her and Reed talking, she knew just how suspicious that must have looked.

The truth was, she didn't care what the butler thought, or Olivia, especially now that she was aware of the situation between Olivia and Reed.

Deep down she had her own worries. What use was it thinking these stupid, irrational, crazy thoughts that had suddenly entered her mind?

She had hated Reed Knight, and for good reason. And now all of a sudden she was harboring these not-so-sweet thoughts about him? Now her breathing hitched each time he walked past, and she chewed her lip whenever he looked at her with those glittering blue eyes.

It didn't matter that her insides were ruffled, or that her nerves jangled whenever he was around. Nobody had managed to raise her heartbeat without laying a finger on her before, and here she was, exhibiting mild symptoms of a panic attack each time she was in a conversation with the man who was her boss.

She was a *maid*.

He was old money. Good, old-fashioned, privileged money.

She was from the wrong side of the tracks, she was what people called trailer trash, if Starling Bay had been that type of town. It was ludicrous that someone like Reed could make someone like her feel the way he did. But he had, and she hadn't imagined any of it. Something invisible and electric, something she could not control, had reeled her towards him.

The only saving grace in all this was that Olivia wasn't in the picture, and hadn't been for a while.

As if anything could ever come of this.

"What are you doing?" Shay cried, as Jenna pulled out one of her hairpins.

"I look too made up."

"You look beautiful." Shay snatched the hairpin from her and slid it back into place.

"I'm not supposed to look beautiful. I'm supposed to look invisible. I'm the maid," Jenna grumbled.

"That's the last thing I ever expected to come from your mouth. What happened to the 'they think they're better than us' bravado?"

Jenna now often wondered this herself. What had happened to her and the way she now saw Reed?

"You, Cinders," declared Shay, pointing the comb at Jenna like a wand, "Shall go to the ball and catch yourself a prince tonight."

Jenna laughed off the suggestion. "You're too funny."

"Dressed like that you're going to catch something."

"A cold, maybe."

"Rourke Halloran's going to be there, isn't he?"

Jenna lifted her eyebrow. "So what if he is?" He'd been quite entertaining, if a little too eager, to talk to the other day.

"You have to admit, he's pretty sexy."

"*Sexy* is a matter of opinion." And Rourke wasn't her idea of sexy, not by a mile. Reed in his white shirt and searching gaze, now *that* was sexy.

Reed watched from the sidelines. The house was busy, and the guests had yet to arrive. They would start coming in a couple of hours' time. The catering company and party organizers had turned up and some people had come over earlier to decorate the entrance hall and ballroom with red and silver hearts.

Olivia didn't do anything by halves. If she had her own money this would have been a completely different party.

At least this was going to work out cheaper than a divorce would have further down the line. The cost of hosting a Valentine's Day ball was negligible in comparison.

He was about to go upstairs and get changed, when the door opened and Jenna walked in. She slipped off her coat, and put it away in the utility room, and when she emerged, she was wearing a figure-hugging black dress that hugged her curves like a second skin.

He couldn't look away.

She had her hair up in a classic knot, swept away from her face, and she looked beautiful. He couldn't believe he was looking at the same woman who scurried around in her apron clutching a duster.

One of the servers from the catering company walked past her, and she smiled to acknowledge him. And then she looked up and caught Reed staring at her.

She hesitated before nodding at him. He returned the nod, and then saw Pennington come up to her and lead her away to the kitchen. Reed followed, intrigued.

Pennington had her over in the corner and was pointing to the plates of cold canapes laid out in neat patterns.

"You'll take a tray out and serve before—"

"She's not here to serve the food," Reed said, stepping in.

"But Olivia said—"

"I don't care what Olivia said," he replied tersely. A part of him wondered if it would have made his life easier to have told

Pennington the real state of play between him and Olivia. "You're supposed to be keeping an eye on the security, Pennington, and ensuring our guests don't park on our lawn. You have the guest list, don't you?"

"Of course. I'll go and tend to that." Pennington looked annoyed as he slipped away.

"He shouldn't be telling you what to do," Reed commented, when it was just him and Jenna.

"You look… nice," he commented, when the real word to describe her would have been 'stunning'. The color rose in her cheeks.

"Thank you." She put a hand to her knot. "I wasn't sure if it might be too much."

"Too much?"

"Too un-maid-like."

She wasn't a maid in his eyes. "It's perfect." He looked away, "Just perfect," he mumbled under his breath. Suddenly, it felt strange talking to her here, it seemed even stranger that she was here to work and not as a guest at the party. A part of him now wished she was here for the party, at least that way he would be able to talk to her more.

"How are you feeling?" he asked. He'd been worried she might not show up today. "Pennington said you went home early yesterday."

"I had an upset stomach, but I'm better now."

"Are you sure?" She looked fine, and he was happy that she had showed up, but he wanted to make sure she was fine to work, because it was going to be a long night, and he didn't want her falling sick.

"Yes, I'm fit to work."

His muscles tensed at her reply. "This isn't the usual work. You're not expected to clean anything."

She nodded.

"I guess I should leave you to get on with things. This is the command center," he told her, turning around and surveying the scene of utter and total chaos. The catering staff had taken over and were busy preparing canapes. "And you're in charge. Keep an eye on things, and don't let Pennington dictate what you do."

"How am I going to tell him what to do?"

"I'm sure you'll find a way." He smiled at her, and when she returned the smile, something in his heart lifted. She looked so beautiful tonight. It wasn't the absence of an apron, or that dress. It was something about the way she was tonight; she looked like one of the guests and, he realized, she could be.

She didn't belong here, hidden away in the kitchen.

And then it hit him like a hammer to the head, the realization that she had once come to a party here at the Knight mansion many years ago, and here she was again, still no nearer to being a guest.

"I'll try and remember that."

"He's not allowed to boss you around, only I am." He hadn't meant it as such, but saying that to her sounded like innuendo, and he suddenly wasn't ashamed of it.

He saw the color in her cheeks, and her inability to say anything back as a sign of her reacting to him in a way that she probably wasn't expecting. It gave him a feeling of victory.

"Please make sure the wine is taken from the wine cellar. You'll need to direct the servers to bring up the bottles when we start to run out."

"Yes, Boss."

# CHAPTER 20

"This is quite some party," Dylan commented.

"Thanks," Reed looked around the huge ballroom. They were standing near the DJ's stage. Easy-listening, not-too-loud music played, and the room was still lit up, enabling all the party guests to eat and mingle. There was an energetic buzz in the air and the party vibe was building. It would probably reach a peak later when the dance music started.

"You Knights sure know how to put on an event."

"I had nothing to do with it."

Dylan laughed. "Except pay for it."

"Except that."

"I was wondering how you would outdo the New Year's Eve party in the tent," said Dylan, "but you have, and spectacularly so."

"*She* has." Reed pointed his beer bottle towards Olivia. She had made an art out of mingling with people. "This has been Olivia's brainchild," he replied, and cast his eyes around the room again.

"Who are you looking for?" Dylan asked. Reed turned his

attention back to his ever-observant friend. "I'm making sure everyone's having a good time."

"It's a Knight party," Dylan grinned, before taking a sip of his beer. "*Everyone's* having a good time. Relax," he patted Reed on the shoulder. "It's time you started to have a good time."

"I am." He would be now, especially because he'd just seen Jenna reappear. Every so often she would return to the ballroom and hover around the buffet tables at the back. Only this time, Rourke was sniffing around her like a dog in heat. It irritated the heck out of him. It shouldn't have, but it did.

Dylan followed his line of sight. "If that's Jenna Lawson, I can't understand why you'd turn someone like that away. She is *hot.*" The note of admiration in Dylan's voice didn't go unnoticed.

"You're taken," Reed reminded him. "You shouldn't even be looking at anyone, let alone finding anyone but Merry *hot.*"

"I don't. I'm only making an observation because I've heard so much about this girl you and Rourke keep talking about."

"We don't keep talking about her," Reed corrected him. He was careful about what he said to his friends.

"Well, I was curious to see her."

"And now you have." Reed glanced at Jenna again. With her hair styled that way, her blue-tipped ends were hidden.

Rourke suddenly appeared out of nowhere and started to talk to her. Reed crossed his arms and watched. He could tell by the way Jenna had folded her arms, by the tilt of her head that she was trying to be patient and polite. She had often been like that with him in the beginning.

"Great party, Reed," Merry came up and hugged him.

"Thank you, I hope you're enjoying yourself."

"I haven't been to any Valentine's Day balls, and I didn't know what to expect, but this is amazing," she gushed. "You and Olivia are exceptional hosts."

Reed nodded. "Thank you, but I believe the honor goes to Olivia. She organized all of this."

Merry smiled, and he felt an arm around his waist. Suddenly, Olivia was by his side. "This is a beautiful party," Merry said to her as Olivia tightened her grip around him and leaned in closer.

"Thank you." Olivia's paparazzi-flash smile might have fooled Dylan and Merry but it didn't fool him. She'd spent a ridiculous amount of money on this party, and he'd let her run wild with it.

Right now, he was sure they looked the picture of a perfect couple. In her full-length, bright red satin dress with her hair brushed back, showing off her long sleek neck and those knock-your-eyeballs-out cheekbones, he could see why he had been dazzled by her, and why he might have jumped the gun. She'd looked just as glamorous as when he'd first seen her.

"We should get together sometime, the four of us," Merry suggested to Olivia, and she looked to Reed for an answer.

"That would be great," he replied. "We'll set something up." He hated lying to her, and could only offer a weak smile because he knew that would never happen. He felt uneasy and longed to end the charade. It sapped his soul, keeping up the lie, and he hated being dishonest to his friends and his family.

Breaking the news to his parents would be difficult. His parents were fond of Olivia, and had flown to Manhattan soon after he'd proposed. The distant memory of that evening at the plush hotel in Manhattan seemed like a dream now. It seemed more than surreal, and he sometimes wished it had been a dream; something he could wake up from.

"Darling," Olivia purred. "People are begging for you to make a speech."

"A what?" His gut hardened.

"A speech." She squeezed his waist gently. One of their

friends walked by and caught the tail end of the conversation. "You're making a speech?"

And then it seemed as if everyone around him heard and they were soon chanting, "Speech, speech."

"I really don't think this is appropriate," he hissed back. He disliked being told what to do, and he especially disliked being told to do something he really didn't want to do.

"Of course it's appropriate, darling."

He wished she would stop calling him darling. "I *cannot* make a speech."

Olivia's lips curved up into a wide smile. "Yes, you can, darling."

"Go up and thank everyone for coming," suggested Dylan.

Reed gritted his teeth together, then walked towards the center of the room just as the DJ turned the music down.

"Stage, stage, stage!" His guests chorused, and he reluctantly walked up on stage. The DJ handed him a microphone, just as Olivia walked onto the stage and stood next to him.

The muscles in every part of his body hardened like concrete. He felt like a fraud. Looking out he saw a sea of faces staring back at him.

The crowd hushed, and an expectant silence fell upon him. The crazy idea flashed across his mind. He could come clean now. He could own up, and tell the truth in this moment. But he had to honor his side of the bargain. He'd made a promise to Olivia, and he had to stand by it. Not only that, but it would be unfair of him to end the party on a sour note. With hindsight, he should never have agreed to Olivia's selfish request to go ahead with the ball, but he had, and he had to suffer consequences such as this— making a speech and pretending to be happy while Olivia stood next to him and they portrayed a happy couple in love.

"I…" He hesitated. The words didn't come naturally. He

couldn't go through with it, not with everyone looking at him with smiling faces.

Olivia took his hand and squeezed it. It was the worst thing that could have happened tonight. He turned to her and smiled, then pulled his hand away and held onto the mic with both hands, a movement that didn't feel right, but felt better than entwining his hand with Olivia's.

"I want to thank you all for coming here tonight, to attend the…our…Valentine's Day Ball." Cheers of delight rang out around the crowd. They were boisterous, excited, having fun. So he continued and thanked them, made a joke about the photoshoot, and thanked Olivia. She slipped her arm around his waist just then, making him regret ever mentioning her. Someone yelled something about the wedding, and the crowd cheered, and then someone shouted out, "Kiss, kiss, kiss!"

And all of a sudden he was faced with a crowd who demanded a public show of affection.

He couldn't.

Instead, embarrassed and angry but trying to hide it, he glanced at Olivia, his lips tight, his face hard.

"Kiss! Kiss! Kiss!" everyone cried. Before he knew what was happening, Olivia's face was upturned towards his, and in that moment he knew it would be easier to give in and silence the crowd, than walk away.

And so he dropped a kiss on her lips. A kiss so fleeting, he let himself imagine that it had barely happened.

It satisfied the crowd, and Olivia looked as if she'd won another beauty pageant. But he saw Jenna at the back, holding a tray in her hand, and even though the distance of the ballroom separated them, he could see the shocked look on her face. She rushed away.

Olivia holding his hand wasn't the worst thing that could have happened tonight, *this* was.

# CHAPTER 21

*W*ine. They needed more wine at the buffet tables.

Jenna asked two of the catering staff to come down to the wine cellar with her so that she could oversee them. "Just these," she said, pointing to the wines Reed had instructed.

She waited until they had left, and stayed behind, seeking a quiet place where she could compose herself. Seeing Reed kiss Olivia had made her feel queasy. Here in the coolness of the wine cellar, she reflected on that moment. Rourke had been trying to crack a joke, and she'd been looking at the buffet tables to see what needed refilling. And then Reed had gone on stage and made a speech, with Olivia alongside him, looking tall, slim, and stunning in that bright red dress.

They made a beautiful couple. A striking, gorgeous, beautiful couple. The businessman and the beauty queen.

*Ex beauty queen,* she reminded herself.

She couldn't deny it. Olivia's beauty was timeless. Jenna pressed a hand to her stomach, feeling as if she wanted to throw up. But she hadn't eaten much earlier at home because she had been busy getting ready.

Maybe she was beginning to confuse her feelings from the

past for the boy who had helped her up from the track—a boy who had forgotten all about her. A boy on whose radar she had never registered in the first place. In her foolish youth, she might have wondered about such things, but in her grown up reality she should have known better. She and Reed mixed in different circles, and different worlds, and she was insane for even thinking about him the way she had been recently.

She blamed her confused feelings—a mixture of jealousy and guilt—on the fact that she was overwhelmed by the scale and opulence of the ball.

Either way, she didn't feel right. Her stomach made peculiar motions, and she couldn't face being around people just yet. She fanned her face with her hand, not that it did much to cool her down, and wondered if she had eaten something yesterday that might have upset her stomach.

Closing her eyes, she saw the image of Reed and Olivia kissing again. For a few strange and silly seconds she replaced the image of Olivia with one of herself. Blood coursed through her veins, and her insides churned. It was wrong to react like this; wrong to wonder what it would feel like to be kissed by him, but she couldn't stop herself.

She'd heard them argue, had heard about the engagement, so why had Reed kissed Olivia up on that stage? He wasn't the type of man who would do something because he was told to do it, especially if he didn't believe in it.

But then she recalled that he had agreed to let Olivia go ahead with the ball, even though he was vehemently opposed to it.

Maybe he was confused? Maybe Olivia had made it up to him. Maybe they were together again.

Maybe this was their thing; a rollercoaster relationship. Some couples thrived on drama. It was possible that these two did. It wouldn't surprise her if this on-again, off-again engagement continued until summer, and then they would marry.

She pressed her fingers into her forehead, as if to steady the whirlwind of thoughts that were careening around inside her head. Then, feeling one of the hairpins digging in, she raised a hand to her head and pulled the pin out.

"What are you doing down here?" Reed's voice jumpstarted her heart.

She looked up to find him walking towards her. "I…I came down with the servers to make sure they picked the wine you wanted," she managed to reply, while her heart thud, thud, thudded.

"Every time I blink, I see you or the servers bringing up more bottles. Do we really need to refill every five minutes?" He stood before her in his dark shirt, and dark slacks. No tux, like many of the guests. She'd seen the batch of extra party invites lying around in the library, specifying cocktail dresses for the women and tuxedos for the men. Reed had blatantly ignored the dress code.

"We keep running out. Everyone's having a great time and they're making the most of your hospitality."

Everyone was having a great time except for her. She wanted to go home all of a sudden, but she couldn't. She had to stay and watch it, watch *them,* and put herself through this torture in the process.

"This is costing me a small fortune," he muttered. "I didn't even want to have this blasted party."

She was in no mood for conversation and made to leave, but he stood in front of her, blocking her way. "Would you excuse me, please? I need to go."

His face tightened as he looked back at her, his eyes burning into hers. "That was a farce, Jenna. Olivia put me on the spot, and everyone got excited."

"I don't know what you're talking about." She prayed that her voice didn't betray her, that he wouldn't see how much it had affected her. She wanted to run home to Shay, and tell her everything. Tell her how much she had come to think of this man and how painful it had suddenly become to be around him; to have all these feelings which she had to keep hidden. It was slow, drawn out torture seeing him with another woman. Reed Knight didn't belong to her, he belonged to Olivia, and she hated that he did.

"The kiss," he said, holding her gaze, making her heart shudder dangerously. "I'm talking about the kiss." The way he said it made her fear that he could read her mind, and that he knew exactly why she was upset. "I didn't want to do it, like the speech I didn't want to give."

Was he telling her because he could see what it did to her? And if that was the case, why did he care? Why was he telling her this? Her heart started to beat louder than ever. This was a do or die moment. "Why not?" she asked, her courage rising. "You're getting married soon, and it is a Valentine's Day ball. You have to give your guests the romance."

"There is no romance. *You* know that." His face was smooth, his gaze soft, his voice softer.

"Do I?" Why had he come down here and why was he talking like this? She dared to hope it was because he felt the same. His words, his expression, his nearness, it was intoxicating, and she was floating on hope.

"Yes, Jenna, you do."

"It's none of my business," she replied, pulling herself together.

"The kiss meant nothing."

"You're telling me as if I care."

"I saw your face when you walked out."

It was as if she'd been shunted by a bus. She'd rushed out, unable to stay and watch. "I'm working. I'm not here as a guest having fun."

"You looked miserable even for someone working."

He was being bold in his assumption. She would have told him that, except he could read her so well, it frightened her. Pretty soon she wouldn't be able to hide her feelings from him.

Even so, this wasn't right, him and her being down here, talking like this. She didn't feel as if she was talking to Reed, her boss. She felt as if they were equal, a man and a woman, with a hint of something dangerous, something not allowed, passing between them.

It wasn't friendship, it wasn't soft and comforting like that, *this* was potent, and powerful, and fiery, and it had the potential to sweep her away if she didn't keep her wits about her.

That was what standing here in the wine cellar looking into Reed Knight's eyes felt like, and she knew, as his eyes glimmered under the lights and bore into hers, that she was powerless to stop herself from being reeled in. In that instant, her gaze dropped to his lips, and she wondered what they might feel like pressed against hers.

She forced herself to look away, because the thought was wrong.

So, so, so wrong.

Her heart was racing and felt as if it was going to explode. She tried to go around him, but dropped her hairpin by accident.

He bent down, then picked it up, staring up at her from the floor. A breath escaped her lips at seeing him at her feet, looking up at her. She felt queasy, and then weak as he stood up slowly. She didn't have it in her to move back, even though her brain was telling her to.

"I saw you talking to Rourke," he said, handing her the hairpin, "and I didn't like it."

"He was talking to me, that's all."

"I didn't like it."

She slid the hairpin into place, and saw him watching her.

"That bit there," he said, leaning forward as if he was going to touch her hair. "You need to…" He made a motion with his hand, and then, when she looked at him in total shock, and confusion, he smoothed her hair down. It was a gentle motion, as soft as a feather, when he put her hairpin back into place then moved his hand away. Her skin prickled and her heart was on full throttle, with enough propulsion behind it to launch a rocket into space.

"Why did you do that?"

"I'm not sure."

He stared into her eyes, and her knees weakened. "Maybe because I wanted to."

A tsunami of emotions swirled around in her mind. Blood coursed through her body. She wanted to ask him, *why?* But something told her that this was a surreal moment, one that she wouldn't be able to make sense of yet, even if he gave her an answer.

"That's an amazing dress, by the way."

The air whooshed right out of her body, but she managed to reply. "Your fiancée's dress is amazing."

"She's not my fiancée."

"Everyone else thinks she is."

"Everyone else is in for a shock."

They would be. She wondered how and when everyone would find out, but it wasn't her problem. "I need to get back. Your butler will be wondering where I am." This time he moved out of her way but only slightly. She misjudged and brushed past him, the hardness of his body imprinting itself on her, meshing with the softness of his earlier move.

She was more confused than ever and barely had time to process the burst of emotions she was experiencing, when she found Pennington waiting outside the door.

He speared her with his stare. "What took you so long?"

"I was checking the wine," she replied weakly and wondered how long he'd been standing there, keeping watch.

"Pennington," said Reed, his voice casual and smooth. "Didn't I tell you to stay out of the kitchen?"

"I wonder why," the butler replied, his nostrils flaring.

"He needs to be brought down a peg or four," Reed muttered behind her. She couldn't take it. Him, this, Pennington. All she needed was for Olivia to witness this and she'd be as good as dead.

# CHAPTER 22

Jenna made herself busy for the rest of the night. She stayed away from Reed, away from the ballroom, and away from Olivia, too. Instead, she hovered around the kitchen area. She found it easier to be with the friendly catering employees who she barely knew, and she was thankful for the small talk.

Instead of keeping an eye on the food and drinks around the buffet tables, she sent one of the servers over to check.

It wasn't until 3:00 a.m., until the last of the guests had gone, and the catering company had cleared and left, that she at last sat down on a kitchen stool and rubbed her sore feet.

She saw Reed in conversation with his friends, Rourke and another couple she didn't know. Olivia was still by his side, with her arm around his waist. She tried to analyze their body language and found herself staring too much, and getting irritated. Pennington told her he'd called her a cab home. When it arrived, she gladly left the Knight mansion, grateful to go home.

She found Shay asleep on the sofa with the TV still playing. Even though Jenna tiptoed around the room, Shay woke up as soon as Jenna turned the TV off.

"What time do you call this?" Shay asked, rubbing her eyes and sitting up.

"Time you were in your bed."

"I waited up."

"I can see that. But you should have gone to bed. It's late."

"How late?"

"Way past 3."

"It's Sunday tomorrow. I can sleep in." Shay re-arranged herself so that she was sitting cross-legged. "So, tell me all about it. How was it?"

"It was a fancy affair," Jenna replied, and proceeded to tell her about the evening, about the guests, and the food, and Olivia's dress. Shay had a million questions about that, too.

"She must have looked stunning in that dress, especially with her amazing figure."

"She did," replied Jenna, not wanting to think about it.

"Did you take any photos?"

"We weren't allowed." Nor had the thought entered her mind.

She proceeded to tell her friend everything, except for what had taken place in the wine cellar, because she still wasn't sure about *that*. She needed to process it slowly, in silence.

Reed telling her that he didn't like her talking to Rourke? That was huge. A part of her wanted to believe that there was a reason behind him telling her, a reason why he had sought her out in the wine cellar.

But another part warned her that Reed was changeable, that she needed to be careful, that he was confused, and she was reading too much into the events of the night.

"What was Rourke wearing?" Shay asked.

"Rourke?" she asked, confused, because her mind was still so wrapped up in Reed.

"Yes. Rourke."

"Why?" Jenna tried to gauge her friend's interest. "Do you like him?"

"He's gorgeous, what's not to like?"

"He knows he's gorgeous," replied Jenna. He also fancied himself as a bit of a ladies man.

"And so he should, because he is."

Jenna double-blinked at her friend. "You really like him? He was a jerk at school."

"Reed Knight was a jerk at school, but you seem to have changed your opinion of him."

"You should stay away from people like Rourke," Jenna told her. "They're not worth the time."

"I'm admiring him from a distance. It's not like I'm going to do anything about it. Who did he come with?"

"Nobody, as far as I could tell." Jenna didn't have the heart to tell her friend that Rourke had been trying to chat to her at every opportunity.

"Were Reed and his fiancée all over one another?"

"They forced him to make a speech, and everyone wanted them to kiss, so they did."

"Aww! That's so romantic."

Jenna said nothing. The kiss still made her stomach churn.

"I'm not surprised Reed fell for someone like that," continued Shay. "She's a stunner."

"I suppose she was, if she won Miss Wisconsin."

"When is the article on their fairytale romance being published?" Olivia's newest fangirl asked.

"I have no idea." She was growing increasingly tired of the conversation. She didn't care to see photos of Olivia Sykes in ten different outfits, gushing about her love for Reed.

Try as she did, she couldn't stop thinking about his words, about the way he'd looked at her, and the way he'd touched her, even if it was just to slip the pin back into her hair. How had that even happened? It should *never* have happened, and yet, and yet she hadn't felt threatened by it. Hadn't felt as if he was making a pass at her.

Or had he?

She scratched her neck as the doubt stabbed her. She hadn't *hated* his actions. Hadn't been repulsed by them, or by him. Surprised, yes, shocked, yes, but not in a stay-away-from-me-you-creep kind of way. Reed had drawn out her feelings from way-down-deep inside her; feelings she had tried to suppress, changed feelings of the way she now saw him. It had started off as her feeling sorry for him, at first, but recently, that concern had turned to something else. A flutter in her belly each time she saw him cemented that.

"You've gone quiet," Shay observed. "I thought you would have tons to tell me."

"I was working," Jenna replied, as if that would explain everything. Then, "Who was he seeing before?"

"Who, Rourke?" Shay asked, clearly obsessed.

"No, Reed."

"Haven't got a clue. Why?"

Jenna picked at the wisp of hair on her dress. "I was curious, that's all."

"Rumor has it that Olivia Sykes swept him off his feet," Shay continued. "He only met her last summer."

Jenna pressed her lips together. "That was fast," she agreed, and then wondered what tomorrow would bring.

Would theirs be a broken engagement tomorrow, or would it be back on?

Reed had spoken to her as if they had something between them. It had been a bold move, a daring move, a move that she would never have made; she knew her place, and as much as she hated thinking like that, as much as she had hated working for him in that damned Knight mansion as his maid, these boundaries had meaning in his world.

But tonight, he had ignored all of that.

*I saw you talking to Rourke. I didn't like it.*

"Do you think he's a player?" she asked, her voice turning wobbly.

"Rourke?" Shay was already nodding her head. "Yes, DUH!" As if it was a given.

"I meant Reed."

Shay's eyes opened wide. "Why, was he flirting with someone?"

"*Would* he flirt with someone?" Shockwaves rippled through Jenna's body as this new idea took seed. Had he done it deliberately—making a move on her like that? Men like him, wealthy men with power, used people like pawns. Maybe there was a valid reason for Olivia's behavior and her arguments with him?

Maybe Olivia had seen a side to Reed that she had not.

What if Reed was a player? Or a cheat? Or a flirt? How was she to know any better? She had been content to play out her small fantasies in her head. Hearing that the engagement was off had enabled her to float in the bubble of her newfound feelings for the man, but they had been for her own guilty pleasure, for her amusement, her entertainment, for making her blue days better.

"I wouldn't have expected him to. He's engaged. Reed Knight is as straight and as boring as he comes, even with all that money. There's never been a whiff of a scandal surrounding him in all the years I've been in Starling Bay, not with the kind of parents he has." Shay fixed her with a questioning look. "Unless you've got something to tell me?"

Jenna shrugged. "He didn't flirt with anyone. He only had eyes for Olivia."

"That sounds about right. Olivia Sykes has given that man a

bit of pizazz. Unlike his friend Rourke, Reed isn't known for making waves and for someone that rich, he doesn't make headlines. I don't even know who he dated before Olivia."

It should have made her feel better, but she knew that regardless, she was in for another sleepless night. "Time for bed," she said, rising from the sofa.

"Your twist stayed in place," Shay remarked in admiration.

Jenna lifted a hand to her hair. "It did."

"Aren't you glad you wore your hair up?"

She was extremely glad. "It worked out well. Looked good too." She smiled. "I didn't feel so out of place among all those finely dressed people."

# CHAPTER 23

Sunday passed in slow motion. The laid-back mood in the house the next day made time crawl.

Olivia's female friends were staying with her at the condo, while the couples were staying at The Grand Hotel. She had been busy entertaining them all and he had cried off that he was busy.

He hadn't had to deal with her, thankfully.

The only event that had been of any significance was that Cecile had returned. He had been happy to see his beloved cook return, and had been pleased to hear that her sister was making a good recovery. He gave Cecile Sunday off, and told her to ease back into work slowly.

On Monday morning, he was back to normal, even though he was fully aware that his life was going to change big-time beginning now.

Jenna knocked on his door to let him know that his snacks were ready, and he leapt up, wanting to see her again, but when he opened the door, she had already disappeared.

At the end of the party he had been trapped with his friends, unable to get away and talk to her, even on the harmless premise of thanking her for working. Olivia had been stuck to his side like a leech, anyway. He'd been grateful to Pennington for calling Jenna a cab home.

But now he had a legitimate reason to be in the kitchen with her. Only, he walked in and found no sign of Jenna, only Cecile.

"You missed my cooking, didn't you?" Cecile asked.

"I *would* have missed your cooking, but between Fellini's take-outs and Jenna's snacks, I had enough sustenance to keep me going." He looked around and saw the snack and smoothie which Jenna had left for him. "You've met Jenna?" he asked, reaching for his plate.

"I have, and I like her. Blue hair?" Cecile grinned. "It gets her noticed, for sure."

"Eye-catching, isn't it?"

"You never told me you were partial to rolls or sandwiches."

"You never asked."

"Hmmm. Now that I know, I'll make sure I continue."

"You don't have to do that," he said hastily.

"Jenna insisted."

"She did?" His hopes plummeted. He had been anxious to talk to her, to find out how she was. Saturday night had been a lot of things, but he hadn't been prepared for that moment when he'd had Jenna to himself. He had acted on his feelings, and it had surprised him. That moment together in the wine cellar had been weighted with something deeper, something he was still trying to understand.

"She did. She said she'd make today's snacks, because she didn't know I had returned and she'd already bought the food."

"I see." He didn't like the sound of that.

"She's nice. She's down-to-earth. Got no high-falutin' airs and graces about her, that *some* people do."

He shook his head and watched Cecile wipe down the countertops. "She doesn't."

He bit into his roll and chewed. After a while, he spoke up

again. "You don't have to wait for your sister to have an operation before you go and visit your family, Cecile."

"I know."

"I mean to say, you're free to take your vacation whenever you want"

"I know that."

"It's good that your sister is walking around and can do things for herself, but you can spend quality time with her instead of only visiting when she's recovering from an operation or an illness."

"Are you trying to get rid of me, Reed?"

He stared at the roll he was holding. "Of course not. On the contrary, it's nice to have you back, Cecile. I missed you."

She eyed him suspiciously. "I don't believe that for one moment."

He snorted. "You should, because it's true."

"I'm making your favorite for dinner tonight."

"Southern fried chicken?" he asked, starting to salivate at the thought.

"You know it."

He smiled in appreciation, and drank his smoothie. The doorbell rang and Cecile walked off to answer it, while he returned to his study with the remainder of his food. There were some important documents he needed to read over.

A few moments later, his door opened, and then came a knock, followed by the sound of Olivia's voice. "Mind if I come in."

"Sounds like you're already in," he muttered, hating the way she often did that. "Don't you know you're supposed to knock first, and then see if I answer?"

"Are you still angry about the speech?" she asked, sliding her pert bottom onto his desk.

"It's done. You're on my paperwork," he said crossly.

"I'm sorry." She pulled out the paperwork and placed it to the side, but remained where she was. "The house is back to normal," she commented.

"The caterers did a great job of cleaning up, and Pennington oversaw everything. You know what a stickler he can be for getting things done."

"And your maid?"

He looked up, detesting the way she'd said 'maid', and wondered if there might be an ulterior motive behind it. "What about her?"

"What did she do?" asked Olivia, pulling off her gloves one finger at a time.

"She doesn't work weekends."

"But she worked on Saturday night."

"Because I asked her to." He wondered if Pennington had mentioned anything else about that night to her, and then he reminded himself that it didn't matter what Pennington said or thought regarding Jenna. There were more important things to deal with. "Have you told your friends?"

"About?"

He ground his teeth together. "You know perfectly well what. About the wedding being off," he said, clarifying.

"I was waiting for you to tell me how we were going to do it."

"We need to make the announcement today, Olivia, as soon as possible."

"Today?" she asked, shocked.

"Yes today," he replied wearily. He had been expecting this, another excuse from her, and further reasons to delay. "The ball is over. We let our friends think that we were still together. I don't want to keep up the pretense any longer."

Her eyes turned sad. "We still have a chance to make it work."

No. No, they didn't. He didn't want a chance to make it work.

"We can't be together, Olivia, you know that. Stop playing games. We had an arrangement."

"I love you, Reed."

He hated the desperation behind those words. "You love the life I can give you. They're two different things. We should do it today," he stated matter-of-factly. "I'll tell my parents, and you can tell yours, and then we'll tell our friends—"

"You've got it all figured out," she said slowly. "And you don't even look sad."

"I have been sad, Olivia. I *am* sad, but we have to do the right thing. Getting married isn't the right thing. We both know we're not right for one another."

"So this is it?"

"We agreed it would be."

"We didn't agree. You suggested that—"

He gritted his teeth. "I gave you what you wanted; a launching pad for your career. I went through with your demands. Can't you find it in you to go through with mine?"

"We're going to tell everyone, just like that?"

"Yes." It had been 'just like that' that he'd proposed to her, so, yes, the breakup could be just like that, too.

"I need a few days."

"A few days?" He didn't like the sound of this. "You said as soon as the photoshoot and the ball were—"

"I know I did. But this is so final, Reed, please. I'm only asking for a few more days. All of my possessions are here, and I still have most of my clothes and jewelry here. I'll need time to pack it all up."

How could he refuse? "Fine." Then, "You never did like staying here much anyway."

"I…I would have gotten used to it in time."

He wasn't so sure. "You hate this house," he reminded her.

Something told him that a lot of their married life would have been spent apart.

"I don't hate it," she said slowly.

"But you prefer the luxury condo, away from me?"

"You said I was in the way, that you couldn't work."

"I expected you to understand and not have your friends come to stay for half the week, every other week."

"You're the one who suggested I move to Forest Heights."

"Because I am a business man, at the end of the day, and I need to work. I had to find what worked for me, since you were too busy enjoying yourself."

The problems between them had started long before they'd reached that point though.

"I'll only need a few days to get everything together, please let me?" she asked.

"Yes," he replied with a sigh. Olivia moved off his desk and clip-clopped out of the study, leaving him in the peace and solitude that he craved.

Once again he felt as if he hadn't moved forward much at all. With Olivia still in the picture, and the world still believing they were heading for a beautiful wedding, he pushed all thoughts of Jenna to the side.

He didn't need the extra complication of sifting through the fog, trying to unravel what it was he felt for Jenna.

# CHAPTER 24

The infamous Cecile was back.

Jenna liked Reed's elderly cook and found that she had a warmth and softness about her that the butler didn't. Pennington had introduced the two women as soon as Jenna arrived. She had been relieved not to see Reed around the kitchen.

Lately, she noticed that he would often be in the kitchen working when she arrived. She had quickly fixed his snacks, knocked on his study door to tell him, but instead of returning to the kitchen, like usual, she disappeared upstairs to get on with her cleaning chores.

She wanted to stay out of Reed's way. After the emotional turmoil of the ball, she'd stayed in bed for most of the day, or rather, lounged around on the sofa, her makeshift bed at night. She had needed to collect her thoughts, to analyze each word that had passed between them and try to make what she could of that episode.

But it was all so unclear, so hard to grasp, and nobody but her understood how things were between Reed and Olivia, and nobody besides her knew that the engagement was off. No one would understand about these feelings she was starting to develop for the man who was her boss. So she kept it all inside her, contemplating that night and trying to make sense of it all.

When she had taken on the job of a maid in the Knight mansion, she had never envisioned the hotbed of emotions she would become embroiled in. This was supposed to have been a simple cleaning job, and yet being around Reed, suffering Pennington's disdain, feeling inferior to Olivia, wreaked havoc with her mind.

Each day was getting harder, and she wasn't sure how long she could put up with it. Life had seemed easier when she had just been broke. She wasn't broke anymore now that she had some money coming in, but *this*, being emotionally torn and confused, this was a dark place to be in.

She was dusting a bookshelf in one of the bedrooms, when she heard Olivia's voice behind her.

"Hi there."

Jenna spun around, surprised to see Olivia not only here at the Knight mansion, but talking to her.

"Hi." She stopped dusting, her instincts kicking in as she braced herself. Had Olivia found out about Saturday night?

"I was wondering if you could give my rooms a quick clean."

Jenna stared at her in shock, and relief. She hadn't been expecting this. But she was also wary. Reed had told her not to touch Olivia's rooms. He had made it a point to tell her that that section of the house was off-limits to her.

But if Olivia had specifically asked her to clean them... "Uh, sure." Jenna glanced back at the bookshelf, weighing up what to do, and wondering what had brought this on.

"I...I..." Olivia seemed to falter, and her not-so-confident demeanor made Jenna wonder if she and Reed had finally decided to go their separate ways. "You might have worked it out yourself," she managed, finally, "but things aren't working out so well between me and Reed." Jenna couldn't believe that Olivia was confiding in her. She couldn't speak. "I…I'm going away for a while," Olivia continued.

*A while?*

The silence dragged out unbearably, so that Jenna was forced to say something, even if it was a lie. "I'm sorry, I had no idea."

"I want to do the right thing by Reed," said Olivia. This was starting to make Jenna feel uncomfortable. She didn't like Olivia opening up to her like this. It was easier having Olivia be the way she had always been in the past with her—cold and nasty. Jenna could handle her better if she was *that* Olivia. Not this one.

Wariness crept over her. "Reed told me not to touch those rooms."

"That's because I told him I didn't want anyone touching them, but you've been here a while now, and he seems happy with you, as does Pennington."

Jenna's eyes widened.

"So, I'm happy for you to give them a quick clean. If you could do it today that would be great. I…" Olivia looked down at the floor, and looked suitably heartbroken, "I don't want Reed to be even angrier with me."

Jenna watched the superficial display of emotions with a calmness that surprised her. "I can give your room a quick clean, if you want," she said. She knew Reed had been eager to make the announcement of a split, and she figured this was the first step.

"He didn't like me staying here."

Jenna's head jerked up. She must have looked surprised, because Olivia continued. "Reed said I got in the way, that I made too much noise and that he couldn't work."

That was what Reed had told her. Olivia wasn't lying. "Okay," she said, not wanting to hear any more, but not wanting to be rude and not say anything.

"I only had my friends stay over a few times, but you know how uptight he can get."

"No, I…I don't know," replied Jenna truthfully. She was eager to leave but Olivia looked as if she was going to cry. She dabbed at the corners of her eyes. "He wants a break and it's come as a huge shock to me. I asked him if we could try to work things out, but he was adamant that we couldn't." Olivia paused, but Jenna wasn't going to give her the surprised reaction she seemed to be waiting for.

"I'm sure you'll work things out," she offered.

Olivia sniffled. "I'm sorry. I don't know what's come over me. This isn't like me."

*Absolutely right,* thought Jenna. This isn't you at all. *What are you playing at?*

"I begged him to at least give me a few days so that I could get my things together." Another pregnant pause followed.

"I see."

"Could you…would you mind dusting the surfaces? I don't want my belongings to get dirty when I'm packing."

Jenna was glad to have something to do other than to stand here and listen and pretend she felt sorry. "I'll start now."

# CHAPTER 25

His father had called him out of the blue and wanted to know about the old movie theater.

"We start work on it next month," Reed informed him.

"I'm mighty proud that you won that proposal, son. Your mom and I loved that place. We have a lot of fond memories of it.'"

"Well, I aim to keep it all old-style, the way it used to be."

"That's the way to do it, son. Don't go turning it into another modern-day monstrosity; we have enough of those clinical glass and iron buildings. A movie theater's supposed to look inviting and cozy. It's supposed to be an event, going to the movies."

"I hear you, Dad." Reed had many ideas for keeping it vintage. "Hopefully you and mom can come out and see it when it's done." He was about to add that he was thinking of making a trip to visit them, maybe sometime next week, when his father asked him, "Where are you with the wedding plans? Have the two of you settled on a honeymoon destination yet?"

"Not yet."

"No? What are you waiting for? Children?"

Reed swatted the back of his neck. "Of course not, dad. These things take…time."

"Deciding where to go on your honeymoon?"

"I've been—we've been really busy here lately. You have no idea. Olivia had a magazine company over to do a photoshoot and—"

"A photoshoot? Whatever the hell for?"

"It was something she wanted to do, and then we hosted a ball over the weekend."

"A what?"

"A ball, for Valentine's Day."

"You can do all that but you can't decide on a honeymoon destination? Everything okay, son?"

"Yeah, dad. Everything's fine."

But the silence followed, and it was freighted with heaviness. Reed wanted to tell him. He wanted to get this off his chest. "Do you want to speak to mom?" his dad asked before he could utter another word.

"Sure."

"Let me see if I can find her for you." He heard his father walking around and was tempted to do it, to break his news. Those five little words what would unleash a torrent of shock and emotion danced on the tip of his tongue.

*Olivia and I broke up.*

"She's gone out to tend to the horses. I'll have her call you later, son."

"Sure, dad."

He hung up, then wiped his hands all over his face, feeling as if the weight on his shoulders had just doubled.

What was he doing letting Olivia dictate the pace of events? He'd given her the things she wanted, and he should have had the guts to tell her that they were going to do things his way now.

That was it. Come what may, he was flying to Montana on the

weekend to give his parents a surprise visit. A difficult visit, no less. But it had to be done.

He could feel another headache coming on. But this time there was no hangover to pin the blame on. He needed food, that's what he needed. And maybe he would hear Jenna still clattering away around the house somewhere if he got out of this claustrophobic study. He'd seen her earlier today, but she was going upstairs with the vacuum and he had been about to go upstairs had it not been for Pennington's eyes on him. Olivia had been over again today as well, and he'd thought it best to lie low. Or at least, to avoid being seen talking to Jenna for now.

"You look like a bear with a sore head," Cecile noted as he walked into the kitchen.

"I feel like a bear with a sore head."

"I fixed you some dinner. Sit down and eat. You don't look so well." She placed his dinner in front of him. "Working too hard again?"

"Always." The smell of seafood risotto floated up to him, and he instantly felt better.

"I made extra, for … *Olivia*." Cecile still seemed to have difficulty saying his fiancée's name. "But I see that she already left."

She'd left? This was news to him. Cecile looked at him, and he wasn't sure whether to let on that he didn't know much about Olivia's whereabouts, or comings and goings. Cecile wasn't stupid. He was sure she knew, or at least had an idea about the iciness between him and his *fiancée.*

"She tends not to stick around here until the evenings," he said, taking a bite and silently rejoicing.

"Not even to eat" Cecile asked.

He shook his head. Back in the early days of their engagement, when things had been sweet and good and she had lived here, and when Olivia had been fun to be around, Cecile cooked for them. He and Olivia would eat here in the kitchen, talking and looking over photos of dresses, and menus, and all things wedding related. That had been when she'd lived here, but even when she then moved to the condo, she would still come over, they would still see each other daily, and at least have dinner together. It all seemed liked a distant memory now.

"This is good, Cecile," he said, appreciating the mouthful of seafood risotto. He had missed her food and knew that when all else failed, Cecile's cooking always turned things around, made the day brighter.

"Jenna gone?" he asked casually.

"No, she's still here." Cecile gawked at him silently. Judging him.

"This is great," he said, attempting to make light conversation.

"I know." Her beady eye was still fixed on him and he contemplated on whether to tell her about the state of the engagement.

"I'll be off now," said Jenna, walking into the kitchen with her purse in her hands. She looked straight at him, and he saw the surprised look on her face.

"Hi," she said weakly, then turned away.

"This is the change from the groceries I bought yesterday," she explained to Cecile, lifting the lid of the glass money jar.

"You must be hungry," said Cecile, pulling out another plate. Reed waited, hoping that Cecile wouldn't let her leave without feeding her.

"I'm okay, thanks." Jenna put the lid back onto the jar.

"Are you sure I can't tempt you with my seafood risotto?" asked Cecile, deliberately holding up a ladleful of it not far from Jenna's face.

Jenna stared at the ladle, licked her lips. "I…I'm not …"

"You look hungry to me," insisted Cecile.

"I have to get back. It's getting late."

"Here," Cecile pulled out a plastic container and handed Jenna the ladle. "Take what you want and don't be shy. I've just remembered I need to call my sister and make sure she took her meds."

Cecile left, and Jenna turned her back, getting busy with the risotto

"Why don't you have it here while it's hot?" Reed suggested.

"It's okay. I'd rather get home first."

She still hadn't turned around to face him, and he wanted to see how she would navigate leaving the kitchen without turning around. "Are you avoiding me, Jenna?"

"No."

"Then turn around."

She lifted her head lift up, and put the ladle back in the pot. Her shoulders hunched as she secured the lid, and still she hadn't turned around.

He could see she was being stubborn. "You *are* avoiding me," he challenged, resting his fork on the plate.

"I was getting on with my chores," she said, slowly turning around at last.

"You always get on with your chores but this must have been the first day since you started here that I haven't seen you. I didn't even hear you clattering around. Tell me why you're mad at me."

Her disheveled hair lay around her shoulders. She looked tired, as if she hadn't slept, and he wondered if she'd had sleepless nights for the same reason he had these past few days.

"I was hoping to see you," he said, when she stared at him silently.

"Why?" He looked into her eyes, wanting answers, needing to know if she felt the same way about him as he did about her. "Did you enjoy the party?"

"Enjoy the party?" Jenna let out an exasperated breath. "I was working, in case you hadn't realized."

*Damn.* That was the wrong question to ask. "Right. I mean, I know." He was trying to gauge her thoughts, trying to get a read on her, trying to figure out where they were.

Even though *they* didn't exist.

"I should go."

"Jenna…" He wanted to talk about that night, and touch upon that conversation, but she was giving him nothing. "You're annoyed at me and I don't understand why. Did I…did I do something wrong that night?"

"Have you announced your break-up?" He hadn't been expecting her to come out with that.

"Not yet."

"Not yet." She looked annoyed.

"Olivia says she needs more time, she wants to get her things together, half her stuff is here, the rest is at the condo."

"And then you'll get married in the summer."

"You know that's not going to happen. Why are you asking?" He wanted something from her. Some small sign that he mattered, that he was beginning to matter. He'd given her an indication that she mattered to him, and he was still waiting to see what she had made of that.

"I have to go," she said, not answering his question.

"Jenna." She looked shaky, so he got up and walked over to her. "Hey," he said, softly.

"Let me go, Reed."

He encircled her wrist in his hand, and she tried to back away. "You can't do this. What if Cecile walks in?"

"I'm not going to do anything. I only want to talk. I want to know why you've been avoiding me."

She looked at him in disgust, and it surprised him. This hadn't been her reaction the other night. "Have I upset you?" he asked.

"Let me go." She tried to pull her wrist away.

"Answer me," he said, letting her go.

"You're engaged, and you can't be seen talking to me, not like this—"

Cecile walked in and her expression turned to steel. Reed stepped away, and so did Jenna. It looked suspicious.

"I see you managed to pour the risotto," Cecile said, calmly.

"Yes…thank you," murmured Jenna. She pressed the lid down on the plastic container.

Reed placed his hands on the countertop, not sure what to do. He wanted to walk out with Jenna, but she clearly didn't want him around. And Cecile was watching him with a patrol officer's keen eye.

"I hope you enjoy it, young lady."

Jenna blushed, muttered, "I will," and "thank you," and scurried away.

"Are you going to let that go to waste?" Cecile asked, nodding her head at his almost-empty plate.

## CHAPTER 26

*S*he cycled all the way home, with Cecile's risotto sitting in the plastic container in the basket.

She had wanted the ground to open up and devour her when Cecile walked in and caught her and Reed in that compromising position. They weren't doing anything, like that last time. But, she still cringed just thinking about it.

And Reed. What had he expected her to say? How could she explain why she was mad at him when she wasn't sure herself? When she was still trying to figure out if he'd made a move on her while he was having his on-off-and-on-again engagement.

She was in the worst kind of trouble, stuck in limbo, unsure of Reed's motives, and unsure of her own feelings. If she hadn't been so desperate, she would have quit. But the other jobs wouldn't be enough for her to survive on and Shay had been pleased that Reed had given her extra hours, and hired her for the party.

If she left now, she would have a lot of explaining to do. The best outcome for all of them would be for Olivia to be nice, for Reed to see how much he really loved her, and for the two of

157

them to get married so that she could forget all of this had ever happened, and move on.

Falling for a man who was engaged, who may or may not have feelings for her, was hard enough without having to worry about the fallout from the broken engagement, or from what society might think if a woman like her took up with a man like Reed.

No.

She did not need this mess.

She'd only recently come out of a bad situation herself. Starling Bay was supposed to have been a fresh new start for her.

She reached home, and propped her bike up against the wall before taking out the plastic container. But something shimmered inside her basket, and she peered closer, not able to see clearly in the dark. It glittered, catching the light from inside the house. She reached in.

And pulled out a watch.

She blinked.

Not just any ordinary watch. This was a Rolex. A fancy Rolex watch with tiny diamonds all around the pink clock face.

*How in the world had it ended up in here?*

Could someone have accidentally left it here, or dropped it while walking past? But, how was that even possible when her bike was at the side of the house and out of the way?

She walked in perplexed, and partly afraid. Shay was on the couch, watching TV and glanced over when Jenna walked in.

"Hey," Shay greeted her.

Jenna quickly hid the watch in her pocket, not exactly sure why she was hiding it when she had nothing to hide.

"Hey," she replied, and rushed into the kitchen. She pulled the watch out again and took a proper look at it under the lights. She heard Shay's footsteps and slipped the watch into her pocket again.

"What's that?" Shay asked, pointing to the plastic container.

"Cecile made me take some risotto. It looks and smells delicious." She opened the lid to show her friend.

Shay took a sniff. "Smells delicious."

"Seafood risotto. Have some with me."

Clearly, Shay had already made that assumption because she'd pulled out two plates.

Hours later, she suffered another sleepless night, full of tossing and turning, but sometime before midnight, it came to her.

It could only be one person. She had ruled out that Pennington had anything to do with the Rolex.

The one person who had always been horrible to her, but had been so uncharacteristically sweet to her yesterday, was Olivia.

Jenna had smelled a rat from the moment that woman had asked her not only to dust her rooms, but when she had started to confide in her about her problems with Reed.

Pennington might not have liked her much, but Jenna grudgingly accepted that of the two, he probably played fairer. He was old-school and old-fashioned, and he clearly hated her blue hair. And while he considered himself above her station, she sensed that Pennington wasn't nasty. Having come to know Reed, she didn't think he would put up with Pennington and all his faults if the man was truly vile.

Olivia, on the other hand, was a snake, and Jenna didn't put it past that woman to do something as devious as to place her watch in her bike basket.

Olivia was trying to frame her, only Jenna was a step ahead, and she wasn't going to let her.

She was determined to show that airhead that she could one-up her.

Unable to sleep, she was up and out of bed before her

morning alarm went off. She was at the offices and the preschool early, as alert as a bunny in spring.

When she finished those cleaning shifts, she went home to shower and nap, but couldn't, and left for her duties at the Knight mansion slightly earlier than usual.

Her heart was hammering when she cycled to Reed's home. The hammering got worse as she propped her bike up against the wall, the way she usually did, the way everyone who ever came to the Reed mansion would have known she did.

Olivia included.

She noted that Olivia's car wasn't parked outside the house today, but she sometimes took a cab here from her condo, so Jenna wasn't entirely sure if she was here or not.

She was therefore extra wary, her nerves antsy as jitterbugs as she let herself into the house. She felt as guilty as hell, even though she had no reason to be.

She hadn't done anything wrong but she couldn't help feel as if she was in the wrong. It was a feeling she hated, just like she hated carrying that watch in the pocket of her skirt.

She saw Cecile's back as she entered the kitchen, her heart sinking. She didn't want to upset Cecile, and she wasn't sure what the cook would think of her after last night.

"Hey, Cecile." She tried to sound like her usual cheery self as she handed over the plastic container which she had washed. "My roommate and I enjoyed every single mouthful of your risotto, thanks."

"That's what I like to hear," Cecile told her. "You're early today."

"I couldn't sleep."

"Couldn't sleep? Any reason why?"

Jenna let out a forced laugh. "I ate too much of the risotto."

"Did you now," said Cecile, in a way that wasn't a question.

"I'd better get on with the cleaning," said Jenna, and walked towards the door, her pulse racing.

"Don't you want to get your apron?"

"Oh, yes. I forgot."

"I washed you some newer ones." Cecile opened a drawer and showed her the pile of folded aprons. "You've been wearing the same old one the whole time."

"Reed didn't tell me."

Cecile sighed loudly. "That man doesn't know much about how to run this house."

"Luckily his fiancée will put that right," Jenna managed to say.

"Over my dead body she will." Cecile laughed loudly, as if her own joke was hilarious. "That woman has never so much as wiped a surface around here."

Jenna stared at Cecile, taken aback by her comments. Had Reed told Cecile about the state of play between him and Olivia?

She couldn't waste time wondering about such things, she needed to concentrate on the task as hand. Quickly slipping the crisp white apron over her neck, she tied it at the back.

"On with the cleaning," she announced, and flashed a smile that belied the anxiety she felt inside. Creeping along the hallway, she looked around for signs of Olivia, and hoped that she wouldn't run into Reed along the way. She couldn't handle any more drama in her life.

She had no idea where the watch went, but she remembered seeing some jewelry boxes lying on one of the dressers. All she had to do was to put the watch into one of those boxes and get out of that room.

Didn't matter if it was the wrong box, she just needed to get rid of the watch. Checking to see if Olivia might be around, Jenna knocked on the door to the room where she'd seen the dresser and prayed that Olivia wouldn't be here.

There was no answer. She turned the doorknob and crept inside.

No Olivia.

All clear.

Rushing over to the dresser, she pulled out the watch from her pocket, while her frantic heart was doing a hundred beats per minute.

She opened the drawers one by one and went through them, looking for a box. Panic crawled all over her skin when she couldn't find a single box.

Had Olivia packed them all away?

She was going to hyperventilate if she didn't find a box soon. Later on, she would wonder why she had been so transfixed with finding a box, why she hadn't just thrown the watch into the one of the drawers.

"What do you think you're doing?" Pennington's voice boomed into the room. She froze. Couldn't get her words out, couldn't find her voice. Slowly, she forced herself to turn around.

Pennington stood there, his vulture-like gaze freezing her to the spot. And then his mouth dropped, and his gaze fell to the watch in her hand. "You thief!" he cried, his eyes wide with disbelief. "You lying little thief."

"No! It's not what you think." She shook her head, then looked at him, with one hand on the drawer and one hand on the watch.

She looked completely guilty.

# CHAPTER 27

Pennington grabbed her arm roughly. "Let go of me!" Jenna screamed.

"Oh, no, you don't. You come right here." His fingers pinched around her arm, and she tried to wrench it free, but he was strong for a man of his age and his slim build.

"Get off!" she yelled. "It's not what you think." But he ignored her pleas and roughly marched her down the stairs.

"I know what I saw, and you can't twist it."

"I can explain."

"Oh, you're going to explain alright, and you can explain it to the cops."

"What?" she cried. He had to be joking. "I know how it looked. Give me a chance to explain."

He'd marched her to Reed's study, dragging out her walk of shame and making her out to be a thief. Her insides lurched, and she wanted to curl up and die when she saw Reed standing in the doorway. He looked dumbstruck. "What the heck is going—" he stopped when he saw her face.

"I caught her stealing this." Pennington held up the watch.

"What?" The shock on Reed's face was like a punch to her stomach.

"I can explain," she cried.

"I caught her in the act, there's nothing to explain. I know what I saw."

"Let go of me," she hollered, and tried to extricate her arms from Pennington's stick-thin fingers.

"Let her go," Reed ordered, his questioning gaze burning into her. She could already tell what he thought, and she didn't like it. He wasn't sure who to believe. He was wrestling with what Pennington had said versus what she was telling him. Disappointment crashed over her like waves on a rock.

"I caught her in Olivia's room, going through the drawers. She had this watch in her hand."

"It's not what it seems, I didn't steal it," Jenna shouted back.

"Shall I call the police?" Pennington asked.

"I didn't steal it. For goodness' sake, give me a chance to explain!"

"Stop it," Reed roared.

"Whatever is going on?" asked Cecile, rushing over. Jenna could see the disappointment in the elderly woman's eyes. It was this she hated the most; that they had already judged her and made their minds up without even hearing her out.

"I didn't do it. I didn't steal it," Jenna insisted.

"Ask her, just ask her," Pennington ordered.

"Were you in Olivia's room?" Reed asked.

"Yes, but—"

Before she could finish, he interrupted, "I told you that her rooms were off-limits. You weren't supposed to clean them. I remember specifically telling you."

She looked at Reed in surprise. This she hadn't expected from him. He stared at her and spoke to her as if she was guilty, as if she'd done the thing Pennington had accused her of, as if he wasn't going to even consider her defense.

"Olivia asked me to dust the room for her, because she wanted to pack," she blurted out.

"Olivia asked you?" She heard the disbelief in Reed's voice.

"Yes, she asked me. Why don't you believe me?" She shrieked. "Ask her yourself and you'll see."

"I'm trying to find out what went on, Jen—"

She cut him short. "You know me. You know I would never do this."

"I told you," said Pennington. "We should call the police."

"I was putting the watch *back*," Jenna explained.

"What?" Reed asked.

"The watch. I was putting it back—and…"

"So you did take it?" Pennington asked.

"No!" She threw an angry look at the butler. "It was in the basket on my bike yesterday."

Pennington laughed. "She's good. She's very, *very* good. Clever."

"Stop it." Reed snapped. "What do you mean the watch was in your bike basket?"

"Exactly that. It was in my bike basket, but I didn't put it there."

"So clever," Pennington muttered, obviously not believing a word of her story.

"I was trying to put it back," she insisted.

"That sounds suspicious."

"Why didn't you come and tell me?" Reed asked.

"Because she's as guilty as hell," said Pennington.

Rage gnawed at her gut and she threw the butler an angry look. "That's why." She flung her hands up in the air. "I knew nobody would believe me. I knew *he* especially," she jabbed a finger at Pennington, "wouldn't believe me."

"But…" Reed let out an exasperated sigh. It told her everything, because he hadn't once said anything to indicate he might be on her side. "Why would someone put the watch in *your* basket?"

"I don't know!"

"Is it Olivia's watch?" Reed asked. The question made her stop and think. She'd assumed all along that Oliva had tried to frame her, but what if it was a perfectly random mistake by someone else? Maybe someone had stolen it from one of the mansions along here and thrown the watch into her bike basket, ready to come back and claim it later?

It was a far-fetched idea, bordering on the absurd, but maybe it wasn't as absurd as the conclusion she had jumped to.

Reed looked the watch over. "I'm not sure if it's hers. I mean," he examined it closely. "It could be."

"Should we call the police?" Pennington asked again.

"Will you cut that out?" Reed snapped. "We don't even know what's gone on."

Jenna started to protest, at the same time that Pennington did.

"Will you stop it, both of you!" Reed shouted.

"I'll leave you all to figure it out," muttered Cecile, and walked off.

"Pennington, can you leave us? I need to speak to Jenna."

"Alone?" the butler asked, as if this was a deadly move for Reed to make. "Are you sure?"

"Don't ask me stupid questions," snapped Reed, then opened his door wider and nodded his head for her to go in. "Do *not* call the police," he said to Pennington.

Jenna waited for him to close the door so that it was just the two of them. Reed turned and faced her and looked at her as if she was guilty.

# CHAPTER 28

The day had turned into a nightmare.

Reed squeezed the soft area under his eyebrow. "Do you want to tell me what's going on, Jenna?"

Her eyes blazed. "You think I did it, don't you?" If looks could kill, he'd be having a coronary.

"I'm trying to get the facts straight."

Her mouth fell open. "Trying to get the facts straight? This is me, Reed," she said, jabbing a finger at her chest. "I wouldn't *ever* pull a stunt like that." Her mouth fell open. "Do you really think I would pull a stunt like that?"

"No, I don't, but I don't know what to make of it."

She looked as if he'd slapped her. "You don't know what to make of it? You don't believe that the watch was in my bike basket when I went home last night?"

He wanted to believe her, and he mostly did but if she had nothing to hide then why hadn't she come to him in the first instance? In his experience, innocent people didn't do sneaky things. He thought he knew this girl—this girl that he hadn't been able to stop thinking about lately—but he wasn't sure anymore.

Maybe, as had happened with Olivia, he was only choosing to see the version of her that he wanted to see, and not the real her?

He had made this mistake before, and as much as he was desperate to believe her, her actions didn't make sense. Jenna wasn't stupid, so if she had nothing to hide why would she sneak upstairs to put the watch back?

Pennington had been with his family for decades. He was old, miserly, and critical, and had a thousand other faults, but Reed knew two things: his dedicated manservant didn't lie, and he would do anything for the family. "I wish you'd come to me this morning, Jenna. I wish you'd told me first."

"And what difference would that have made?" she replied, her voice low as if she was defeated. "You would still have looked at me as if you weren't sure. Am I right?"

"No." He shook his head.

"You're looking at me now as if you're not sure, as if I'm dirt."

That wasn't true. At all. He rushed towards her, but she stepped back. "I'm not looking at you as if you're dirt. I never have, Jenna."

"That's a lie and you know it. The first day I turned up on your doorstep, when I came for the interview, and you stood there...shirtless..." she paused, shaking her head, "And you looked at me as if you thought I was some loser who had come to demand something from you. I know the way you looked at me."

As it was, he couldn't remember that moment too well. But, yes, he remembered being shirtless, and slightly hungover, after a night with Dylan and Rourke. But he didn't remember looking at Jenna as if she had been dirt. "I didn't know who you were, and I had a hangover. I wasn't expecting anyone."

She turned her back to him. "You're all the same," she sighed, "it's always the same."

He moved towards her and placed a hand on her shoulder.

"What do you mean it's always the same? Turn around, Jenna, talk to me."

But she didn't, so he walked around to face her. Gone was the fiery Jenna who looked as if she'd wanted to punch Pennington a few short moments ago. The woman before him now looked as if all life had been sapped from her. "You can't find a good enough logical reason why that watch would be in my bike basket, because you're not looking at it the proper way—from the point of view of someone who hates me."

"Who hates you?"

"Take your pick, it could be Pennington or Olivia or even Cecile."

"Don't be ridiculous."

"You find that ridiculous, yet you find it easier to believe that I'd steal the watch at all, and from Olivia's rooms, when you've cautioned me against going into them. Why would I take such a risk when I know anyone could walk in and catch me?"

He didn't follow. "Pennington did walk in and catch you."

"But I was innocent! I am innocent! If I really wanted to take it do you think I'd do it when Pennington was sniffing around? Don't you think I'd have done it when the photoshoot was going on and everyone was too busy to know what I was up to?"

"So why were you in her room?"

A gasp escaped her lips and a look of disappointment settled over her face. "Because she wanted me to clean her rooms before she packed."

He took her hands in his, and she tried to pull them away. "I believe you. I *want* to believe you completely. I know you would never steal, but Pennington saw you with it in your hands and in Olivia's room, and I'm trying to piece it all together. It's come as a shock, I wasn't expecting all of this today. I have enough fires to fight as it is."

Her hands had gone soft, and limp, and he pressed them

gently, a surge of hope uplifting him. "I'll get to the bottom of this, trust me?" He placed a finger below her chin and lifted it gently.

"Trust you when you don't trust me?" she cried. "I had the watch because I was trying to get one up on Olivia. I thought it was her. It *had* to be. She hates me, and you've broken up, and maybe she saw you and me coming out of the wine cellar that day, and she wanted to make trouble for you and for me. What better way to do it than this?"

"I trust you, but this is a delicate situation, Jenna. I will clear your name, I will get to the bottom of it, but I have to tread carefully." He stared into her green eyes, saw the hurt, the disappointment, and wanted to make it disappear. This woman had suffered enough at his hands, just like the sixteen-year old girl had suffered all those years ago. Difference was, he knew about it now.

It wasn't the right time to figure out where he and Jenna were, what they had, what they could have. It would have been hard enough even if his world hadn't completely upended right now, but he had to get through the initial hurdle of announcing his and Olivia's break-up first.

Something odd was going on behind the scenes, something nasty, and he was going to get to the bottom of this. "Don't look so sad," he told her.

"Easy for you to say. Nobody's ever going to look at you and find you guilty of anything."

She was right. He would never be in this position, even if he had stolen something, people would find a way to explain it. Nobody would ever think it of him, yet someone like Jenna was an easy target. That was what Olivia had thought. He stared at her lips, and her nose, and her eyes, and realized how much he thought about her when she wasn't around. "We'll get through this."

"We?" she asked.

"Yes, *we*. You know that Olivia and I are no more, and we haven't been together for a while. You know that it's all been a farce." He pressed his thumbs into her soft palms, wanting to comfort her. It was hard holding back when he wanted to put his arm around her, and protect her, but he couldn't. It was a battle to restrain himself.

She stared at him. "Sometimes I'm not so sure."

"It's been a farce, and nothing more." He leaned forward, wanting to kiss her, wondering if she wanted the same, but the timing wasn't right. Even though her parted lips were moist and inviting. He was tempted, but he held back, forced himself not to go there.

"I don't know what to make of things," she said, her voice soft. "You and me. I don't know how to be around you sometimes."

"You feel it too?" he murmured, comforted by her words because at least he knew that she was as lost as him.

She nodded. "Sometimes I can't stop thinking about…"

"I can't stop thinking about you lately. Especially since the night of the party."

Her eyes flashed, as if a memory had suddenly ignited. He understood. He felt the same. It had no label, these new feelings he had for her. Things weren't going to be clear-cut, going forward but he wanted to probe, and delve, and explore what they might be able to have.

"I thought it was only me," he said, leaning in as if he was going to kiss her.

"We can't, Reed."

He stopped short, their noses almost touching. "I know," he whispered, "but I am so tempted to kiss you right now, and I know I can't."

He heard her breath hitch, saw her bite her lower lip. "You

drive me insane, Jenna, and for all the right reasons." He pulled back, then kissed her nose. But the door burst open, and they both turned to look.

"Reed?" His father's voice shattered the moment.

"Dad?"

What the heck was he doing here?

# CHAPTER 29

The man she now knew to be Reed's father stared at her as if she was dirt on the sole of his shoe. Jenna pulled away, her heart clattering around in her ribcage like a trashcan in the wind. "Who is she?" he asked.

Nobody spoke.

Next to him stood the woman she presumed to be Reed's mother; she threw Jenna a contemptuous look, making her shrink inwardly. Jenna wished she were invisible, she felt completely wretched at this very moment.

Memories from years ago pierced her like a knife.

"Reed?" his mother asked, her face a picture of shock, but before he could reply, the familiar clackety-clack of those stilettos-from-hell sounded outside. Olivia walked in, looked at Jenna, then at Reed, and put her hand to her mouth, exhibiting shock of epic Oscar-award winning proportions. "I suspected as much," she cried, her lips twisting, her face distraught.

"For goodness' sake, Olivia," Reed growled. "Stop overreacting."

"*Overreacting?*" His mother's voice raised an octave. "She

has every reason to be upset. What's gotten into you, Reed? You're getting married in a few months!"

"What are you doing?" his father thundered, glaring at him. "And who the hell *is* this?" He nodded at Jenna, and her stomach flip-flopped. His voice, his manner, his words, on top of everything that had already happened so far, were too much for her to take.

It had been bad enough seeing everyone's reactions, Pennington, Reed, even Cecile, but now from his parents, too? In a hard and sharp instant she felt as if she was back at Reed's birthday party, tripping up outside his house and hearing the cruel laughter as Shay helped her to get up.

"She's the maid," Pennington replied, appearing out of nowhere.

Jenna blinked, unable to say a word. Her usual feistiness had deserted her.

"You're having an affair with *the maid*?" His mother looked as if she was going to pass out.

"I can explain, it's not what you think," Reed said.

"You don't need to explain, we can see what's been going on."

"No, dad," replied Reed, getting angry. "You have no idea what's been going on."

"Oh, dear lord." His mother fanned her face. "I need to sit down."

"What are you doing here anyway?" Reed asked. "I had planned to visit you this weekend. I was going to surprise you."

"Don't worry about that, you have surprised us," his father replied. Olivia rushed out of the room with a flourish.

"Poor girl," said his father. "I had no idea what she's been dealing with. No wonder she sounded distressed when she call—"

"She called and told you to come?" Reed asked.

"You weren't supposed to mention that," his mother hissed, then rushed out, presumably to pander to Olivia.

Jenna felt hideously out of place, like mud on a white carpet. It was unbearable, being talked about as if she wasn't there, and being made to feel like dirt. She couldn't take it, couldn't stand here and let them look at her like that any longer.

"You're carrying on with the maid, when you have such a beautiful fiancée? Have you gone mad?" his father barked, pacing around the study. He shook his head and mumbled to himself. "The name, the Knight name. Does it not mean anything to you, boy?"

"I haven't done anything."

His father stopped and stared at Reed in disbelief. "You're getting married, have you forgotten?"

"You're not listening to me," Reed ground out slowly. "It's not what you think. You don't know what Olivia is capable of, and when I tell you, you won't believe it." There was an edge of viciousness to his voice; something Jenna had never heard on him before.

It was ironic, she thought, hearing him use the same words she had used earlier when she had tried to get them all to listen to her and see her point of view. She rushed out, unable to listen to this a moment longer.

Even as she left the room, she knew Reed wasn't going to call for her, or try to stop her. He wasn't going to save her, or exonerate her, or speak up for her. He was going to let her flee the scene like a guilty person.

He had wanted to run after her, but it would have made things worse if his parents saw him going to Jenna's defence, and not give an iota for Olivia. He could already hear Olivia's fake tears, and the sounds of his mother soothing her in the room next door.

Things were already hellishly worse, especially with his

parents arriving unannounced. He was convinced that Olivia had put them up to this. She had known they were coming.

And it got him thinking about the Rolex.

"Did Olivia tell you to come?" he asked his father.

"She was worried about you."

That answered his question.

"You didn't answer my question, son. Are you fooling around with the maid?"

"No." He took a breath in. "I might as well tell you. We've broken off the engagement."

His father swept his hand over his face. "You've done *what?*"

"Broken off?" Pennington echoed. His thin lips open like a fish in shock.

"Yes. The engagement is off," Reed replied calmly. "It has been for a while. I wanted to come and tell you and mom this weekend."

"It's been off? For how long?" his father asked.

That was a difficult question to answer. For him, things had soured before Christmas. "Months," he replied tiredly. The entire last hour had drained him emotionally. He thought about Jenna, and couldn't begin to imagine what she must have felt like.

His mother returned. "Is it true?" she asked, looking bewildered. "Olivia says you broke off the engagement?"

He didn't know where to start, and he already knew he had an uphill battle trying to convince them that he was not in the wrong. "I know what you must be thinking."

"You have no *idea* what I'm thinking," his father snapped. "You've ruined the Knight name!"

"Because we're not getting married?" Reed asked.

"Because you're having an affair with the maid!"

His mother looked pale. "Olivia says the maid stole her watch."

"Who stole her watch?" his father asked.

"The maid, who else?"

He hadn't told Olivia that her watch was missing, and Pennington had been in the study the entire time, so Reed knew he hadn't told Olivia. Nobody had told her that the watch had been in Jenna's basket—because he believed Jenna and knew that must have been true. And nobody had told Olivia that Jenna had tried to return the watch to her drawer.

Only the person who had fabricated this entire ruse would know that.

"Pennington, get Cecile to make something for my parents. They've had quite a shock. You should take it easy," he told them both. They looked completely shell-shocked. "I will explain everything to you but I need to deal with Olivia first."

"Answer my question, Reed," his father ordered. "Were you having an affair with the maid?"

"No."

"Do you have feelings for her?"

He couldn't answer that in one word and have them understand. The easiest thing would be to tell the truth, despite how badly it would reflect on him, given the current situation. It would be a while before he could explain to his parents properly.

"Yes," he replied, and saw their faces crumple. His mother pressed a hand to her chest, as if she was having chest pains. He had never seen his father look so disappointed. "I don't expect you to understand, I wouldn't understand it myself if I were in your shoes, but you will understand in time."

"I will *never* understand this," his father said in a quiet voice. Reed stared at his mother, but she looked deflated, as if all the air had been knocked out of her.

"I need to take care of something," he said, moving to leave.

"I think you've taken care of enough."

"Dad, give me time. Just wait." He rushed out and ran

upstairs, taking two steps at a time because the anger inside him needed to be spent.

He found Olivia in her bedroom, packing her clothes, her back turned to him. He slammed the door hard. She jumped.

"Why did you call my parents?" he asked.

"Because I couldn't walk away so easily. I still love you—"

"I don't think you know the meaning of the word. You use people to get what you want, and when they figure you out, you hate on them."

She smirked. "Don't act so high and mighty with me. I'm not your maid. Don't go acting all superior."

"I'm not acting all superior."

"Girls like her like that sort of thing."

"What sort of thing?"

"Having someone powerful, someone with money, give them some attention. It goes to their heads."

"I could say the same of you," he told her, knowing that Jenna was nothing like that. She hadn't done anything untoward, if anyone had, it had been him.

"What were you doing with her in the study?" she asked, and then, without giving him a chance to reply, "I suppose there must have been many moments like this behind my back?"

"No."

"Are you cheating on me, Reed?"

"Don't be so ridiculous," he hissed back.

"With the maid, that would be ridiculous."

"There is nothing going on," he replied calmly. Because there wasn't.

"And that's what I told you about the photographer—"

"The one who was in your apartment in his boxer briefs while you took a shower, the one who stayed the night?"

"On the couch. There was nothing going on, I swear."

"And you're comparing that to me and Jenna?"

"I've seen the way you look at her, and it's not the way you look at me."

He swallowed and said nothing, contemplating her words. He'd tried to keep his emotions to himself, had tried not to show anything, but perhaps he hadn't been as good at hiding his feelings as he thought. "I used to look at you like that, Olivia. I used to feel that way about you—"

"So you do feel something for her?"

"I don't know what I feel for her. I know that it's not what I feel for you, and goodness knows I've tried, Olivia. But it's not all my fault. At least be honest with yourself and admit that. You were never here. You hated living here, you did your own thing. And you want different things."

"I love you and I still want a life with you, Reed."

"You want what I can give you. What good did this do? Having my parents show up like this?"

"Did you think I was going to let you walk away unscathed?"

There it was, the vindictiveness and viciousness, hiding behind a glossy façade. Behind that stunning face and figure, she was nasty inside. He had grown sick of these women who saw his wealth and his status first, and then saw him.

Jenna was a boatload of different. She was another galaxy, another universe, another world. She wasn't a breath of fresh air, she *was* the air, and she allowed him to breathe, where Olivia suffocated him.

Jenna didn't care about his material possessions, about what he had or didn't have. She'd never sought out to gain favor with him, had never tried to impress him in order to get a raise or because of who he was. In fact, she'd always been guarded and wary, and had hated him on sight.

For him, Jenna was the right thing, the best thing, the only thing. And if they were ever going to have anything, he would take it real slow this time.

"You orchestrated everything so perfectly, not just having my parents turn up like this, but the watch."

Olivia's eyes widened as she tried to feign surprise and shock, and failed miserably at both. "I…why…why would you think—"

"Don't pretend, Olivia," he said, irritation crawling over him like a line of spiders. "It wastes my time and makes you look stupid. You put the watch in Jenna's basket thinking Pennington would find it, or you would go crying to him about it. You knew eventually that he would go looking for it in Jenna's belongings."

"Did Pennington find it?" she asked, her eyes gleaming. So that was what she had planned all along? He understood the workings of her mind now, saw what had been her real intention.

Olivia would have mentioned that her watch was missing, and Pennington would have been on the hunt trying to find it. After what had happened with the last maid, it wouldn't have been long before he found it and blamed Jenna.

Only Jenna had known nobody would have believed her, and she'd tried to do the only thing she could to end the matter quickly and quietly.

Pennington catching her in the act had played beautifully into Olivia's hands.

He ignored her question, refusing to give her the satisfaction. "I know it was you, and soon everyone will know it was you. You brought this on yourself, and you have no one to blame but yourself."

"That bland and boring Miss Average has no right," Olivia sniped, pointing a finger at him, "she has no right to a man like you."

"We're not together," he clarified. "We've not even so much as—"

"I don't want to hear what you've done—"

"We haven't done anything."

She gasped, as if he'd punched her. "You haven't kissed her?"

This was not a conversation to be having with an ex, but he answered it anyway. "No." A peck on the nose didn't make for a proper kiss.

"Then how do you know you like her?"

"I just do." Because they had a connection; something hard to describe and put into words. It had been more like a feeling that had grown inside him, and become stronger each time he saw her. Not being able to do anything about it, but admire her from afar, and having tiny moments here and there, magnified the innocent time they did have together.

Olivia didn't seem to understand, and he didn't want to make her understand. His situation with Jenna, as fragile and nebulous as it was, was none of Olivia's concern.

She walked towards him, something in her face he couldn't decipher. A wistful look, he had never seen before. "Do you sometimes think we might have made a mistake?" she asked, running her finger over his lower lip. Her boldness and closeness made him flinch. He grabbed her hand, not too hard, but not softly either, and moved it away from his face.

"We've done the right thing, of that I have no doubt."

"That maid of yours is nothing but a lowlife. A broke, pathetic, lowlife creature."

Those harsh words reflected Olivia's ugliness, and he paid no heed to them. She had already shocked him with the events of today, and he had been astounded by the level of her deviousness. All this, after he had given her what she wanted, the photoshoot and the ball, and instead she had done her level best to inflict as much pain on him and Jenna as she could.

But now that he knew Jenna felt the same, there was no way he was going to be able to hold back. He was in a messy situation, and it was pointless to think of the future when his present was so complicated, but he was determined to find a way forward.

There would be talk in the town. He didn't care about himself but knew that Jenna would be painted as a homewrecker. All he could think of was how to protect her.

As for Olivia, he would have the last laugh, and he would seek revenge on Jenna's behalf without her knowing a thing about it.

# CHAPTER 30

The hours seemed to stretch out for a day, and she braced herself when she heard Shay finally come home.

"Hey," said her friend, taking her shoes off and collapsing into a heap on the sofa. "You're home early."

"I quit."

Shay bolted upright. "Quit what?"

"Being a maid for Reed Knight."

"What? Why?"

"I couldn't take it anymore."

Shay's eyes widened revealing lots of white. "You can't quit just like that, Jenna. You have to go through the agency." She looked at Jenna with suspicion. "What did you do?"

"Why does everyone think it was something I did?"

The look on Shay's face turned worrisome. "How bad is it?"

"It will sound bad, but it isn't *that* bad."

Shay angled her head. "Tell me."

"Okay, but bear with me and don't judge me. I quit because… ugh." She didn't know where to start. "So much has happened…I don't even know how to begin."

"Start at the beginning, and tell me everything because this isn't going to go down well at work. Reed Knight is a big deal in this town, and to lose his business isn't going to reflect well on the agency."

"You didn't lose his business, I quit. You'll have to find another maid."

"Tell me now before I find myself another roommate."

So she did. She told Shay everything to the best of her knowledge, except that she didn't tell her about her and Reed.

She told her that Reed and Olivia had broken up, and then about the watch and how she had tried to put it back and how the butler had caught her. She told her about her and Reed being in the study when his parents had walked in.

"Whoa, whoa, whoa," said Shay, standing up and holding her head as if it was going to explode. "Information overload."

"I told you it was a lot."

"You've been doing *all this?* You were only supposed to be cleaning."

"I haven't been doing anything. I have been cleaning," she replied, feeling defensive. Only, Reed did feel something, she knew that now. It gave her strength, but it also made her mad that he had stood by and not said anything in her defense.

But could he have?

She'd experienced his parents first hand now, and could see how hard it was for Reed, how hard it was going to be.

And the mess.

The huge, sticky, complicated mess that now surrounded them both, especially if his parents believed what they had seen.

"So, they broke up?"

"Yes, they broke up."

"But the ball was only last week."

It was going to take a while to explain, and for Shay to

understand it. It made her see the huge battle Reed had in trying to explain the situation to his parents.

She shuddered at the thought of how they had made her feel, told her there was no future in it, no matter what Reed said. She didn't want to be involved with a man whose family thought she was dirt. As it was, she'd spent her life thinking she was no good, thinking that waitressing and doing odd jobs were as good as it was going to get. But she'd seen Olivia, seen how someone nasty and with no-good intentions but a glossy façade could go so far. And even then she had still managed to mess things up spectacularly.

"He did that because he felt bad. He gave her the photoshoot and the ball but they broke up weeks ago. I don't think they even had a relationship for months. She lives in her condo, and he buries himself away in his study. They barely see each other and the few times they did, they argued. I should know because I overheard them."

"Why didn't you tell me sooner?"

"Because it didn't feel right to tell anyone. They didn't *tell* me, it was a conversation I overheard."

Shay looked astounded. "We're friends, and this is gossip! Hot gossip, from one friend to another. It wouldn't have hurt you to tell me."

"I didn't want to gossip."

"Why not? These people aren't your friends, you've told me before you couldn't care less about them."

"Reed's your client."

Shay looked at her. "And you're my friend. Tell me something, why would Olivia plant the watch on you? And you quitting. It doesn't make sense. Is there something else you want to tell me?" she asked slowly. "Because it feels to me like there is."

"We didn't do anything."

Shay slapped a hand to her face. "I can't believe I'm hearing this. You wouldn't say that unless you had something to do with it. Tell me you weren't the cause of their break-up?"

"I wasn't."

"It doesn't add up, Jenna."

"Hear me out."

"Gladly, but please don't give me a heart attack."

"I won't. They were over well before I even started to do nice things for Reed."

"Do nice things for Reed?" The color drained from Shay's face. "What kinds of *nice* things?"

"Like making sandwiches and smoothies for him. I already told you. And I might have made him a couple of easy-to-cook hot meals, too."

Her friend looked confused. "You're a *maid*."

"I felt sorry for him. He asked me to make smoothies, and I felt sorry for him so I would fix him snacks. What are you looking at me like that for? I billed my hours on my timesheet, you got the extra hours for me doing that." She couldn't help but smile at herself. "He liked my snacks."

"Why do I get the feeling that it's the snacks that got you in trouble?"

"It wasn't the snacks."

"But you felt sorry for him?" Shay asked.

"Because Olivia was so nasty to him. She used him to further her career, and she says she loves him but it sounds to me as if she tried to use him as much as she could. The way she treated him wasn't love. You weren't there, Shay, you didn't hear the arguments. I felt sorry for the guy. I think he really wanted things to work out."

"And why are you quitting? If it's just the watch and Reed

believes you, and this Olivia creature is as vile as she sounds, the truth will come out."

Jenna exhaled and sat forward, propping her elbows on her knees in despair. "Because she lied and made it seem as if Reed and I were having an affair."

"And why would she say that?"

"Because she's a neurotic psycho."

Shay's brow furrowed. "When you did those extra hours for the ball," she said, quietly, "you looked amazing. Oh, my goodness." She got up and started to pace around the room. "You made such an effort with your hair and getting ready, and you were worried about looking too sexy…"

Jenna looked up at her friend guiltily.

"You like him, don't you?" said Shay slowly. "You used to hate him at first, but then…the bike."

"He lent me a spare one."

"That should have alerted me."

"He was being nice!"

"Exactly! "cried Shay. "Goodness, Jenna. When I asked you to rewrite the story of your life, I didn't mean for you to steal another woman's fiancé!"

Jenna jumped up. "I didn't steal him. She wasn't his by that time."

"Something did happen, then?"

Jenna swallowed. "No, it didn't." How was she to explain what had happened in the wine cellar, or this morning in the study, when nobody but she and Reed would understand the river of emotions that had swept over them? "I swear nothing happened." Nothing much. Nothing *serious*.

"It doesn't add up," muttered Shay. "You're not telling me everything."

"How can I tell you when I'm not even sure myself?"

"Did you two ever kiss?"

"No." *Not properly.*

"Almost kiss?" Shay asked.

"No." He'd brushed her nose. That didn't qualify as a proper kiss.

"Hold hands?"

"We…we like each other."

Shay looked as if she'd taken a pin out of a grenade. "You like Reed Knight, and now his engagement is over, and you've both been doing nice things for one another."

"Harmless things," Jenna clarified.

"Jenna, what have you done?"

"Nothing! I've done nothing."

"Then why are you quitting?"

"Because you don't know what it felt like to have his parents stand there and judge me."

"His parents have every right to be shocked if this is the first they've heard. I'm shocked, I'd been expecting this huge, fancy Knight wedding in the summer, and I'd been looking out for the magazine issue of the photoshoot. *I'm shocked.* So I can't imagine what they must be feeling. And besides, once they go back home and everything settles down, there's no reason why you can't go back and work there."

"I can't."

"Why not?"

Because she was confused about Reed, and the way in which he hadn't defended her, and the way he'd let everyone talk about her as if she was the guilty one.

"You need the money, Jenna. And I could do with my boss not breathing down my neck about it."

"I can't go in, please, at least not while his parents are around."

"I'll try to contain the situation at work. I guess, if they don't know that you quit, and Reed probably has enough drama to tend with for now, then you can just lay low for a day or so."

"I'll still do the other two jobs."

"I hope so, because when *this* news breaks, my boss isn't going to be too happy. I won't be able to offer you any other positions."

# CHAPTER 31

"I've lost my appetite," his mother stated.

"Mom, please. Try and eat something."

"I had a big breakfast, Reed. I'm not hungry."

His parents had barely picked at the light lunch that Cecile had fixed for them.

After dinner last night he had sat them down and talked to them at length here in the dining room. He'd told them about how things between him and Olivia had broken down, and how little time they had spent together, and of her desire to revive her flagging career.

Out of decency, he hadn't mentioned anything about the photographer. Yet, even having said all that, he couldn't help but feel that the news was still too shocking for them to absorb.

His parents had been up early today, but, unlike the other times when they came to stay, they hadn't yet set foot outside. He let it go and wondered what his parents were going to do today. His father had his nose in the newspaper. The conversation last night hadn't ended too well, with his father asking him if Jenna's interest in him might be related to his wealth.

He'd just explained to them how things had been with Olivia, but clearly this hadn't sunk in. This was what Jenna had been trying to tell him, that people assumed she would be the one who was at fault, simply because of her status.

His mother sat quietly at the table, and he didn't know how to turn the mood around.

Olivia had gone, and he was thankful to have one less thing to stress about. Reed lost no time in ensuring that her things were packed and out of the house.

Pennington had helped, and Reed had noted that relations between his butler and his ex-fiancée were muted. He hadn't yet had a chance to talk to Pennington alone to bring him up to speed with things. It wasn't that he was eager to paint Jenna as a saint, more that he was eager for Pennington to see the truth behind Olivia's façade.

On the surface Olivia would have been the perfect daughter-in-law for his parents, with her grace and beauty, but for him, such surface-level things were not important.

He was aware of the battle he had on his hands with regards to Jenna and his parents, and that was without him even knowing what the future held for them both.

He had a feeling that Jenna wouldn't come to work today, not while his parents were around. But then he wasn't sure if she would stay away because of him, too. He hadn't gone after her when she'd run out, and he hadn't even called her. He hadn't had the time because he had talked long into the early hours of the morning with his parents. And by the time he'd gone to bed it had been late.

It was clear that they needed to talk, but a phone conversation didn't seem adequate; he needed to see her face-to-face, and he preferred to do that, but not while his parents were around.

"Maybe dinner at Fellini's might get your appetite back?" Reed suggested, when the silence became too heavy to bear. "Shall I make a dinner reservation for tonight?"

His father put down the newspaper. "Your mother and I had a dinner reservation with Hyacinth at The Olive Tree , but I've canceled."

"You've canceled meeting Hyacinth?" his mother asked.

"I'm in no mood to meet anyone, least of all Hyacinth."

"She won't know yet. Will she?" His mother looked at him, as if he had any control over the rate of rumors spreading in Starling Bay.

"That woman's got the nose of a bloodhound," his father snapped, behind the newspaper. "She's the last person we should be going to dinner with at a time like this."

Hyacinth Fitzsimmons was the town's busybody. Well-respected, feared and avoided by many.

"Then why don't we go to dinner with Reed?" his mother suggested. She looked at him for encouragement.

"Let's go to Fellini's, dad."

"You can't hide behind a newspaper forever, Wilbur."

"My son is carrying on with the maid, Alison!"

"She seemed quite restrained, Wilbur, given that we behaved abominably towards her."

"We had reason to."

Reed was about to say something, but his mother shook her head at him. "Maybe, but we didn't know the truth, then."

His father's hands shot to his lap, the newspaper rustling as it came down. "The truth?"

"What Reed said, the truth about Olivia."

His mother had had time to think. She was obviously starting to see reason. His father huffed, and Reed knew it was going to be a long and difficult process to get him to understand.

"I find it hard to think that she was as nasty as he painted her to be."

"Painted?" Reed threw back. "I'm telling the truth. You won't believe me because you can't see how she could be like that. She is very good at putting on a façade."

"What are you going to do?" his father asked.

"About what?" he cried? The Knight name? Their reputation? These things had been foremost on his father's mind last night.

"About the maid," his father said, stiffly

"Wilbur, I don't think now is the best time to discuss these things. Everything is too raw and unsettled right now."

"Jenna hasn't done anything wrong," Reed stated, feeling defensive. Neither of his parents spoke, which further angered him. He was fed up with their attitude.

"She hasn't," he insisted. "She didn't steal anything and she isn't the reason for the broken engagement."

"But she's a maid, son. And she has blue hair! We didn't bring you up to frequent with the likes of—"

"Dad, stop, please!" Rage simmered in his belly, and he was trying hard not to lose his temper. For the first time in his life, he started to see how life might have been for Jenna, and others who weren't born with his privilege.

"Wilbur, that's enough."

His father shrugged. "I suppose it's not as if he's going to marry her."

Reed banged down his glass of water, making it spill onto the white silk tablecloth. "If I want to marry her, I will."

Where this had come from, he had no idea. He wasn't even sure if Jenna wanted to see him again, judging by the way she'd run out yesterday. He hadn't even checked up on her to see if she was okay, but he wasn't going to let his parents talk about her like that.

"You're thinking of marrying her, Reed?" his mother asked, looking stunned.

"You said there was nothing going on," his father said. "Was there?"

If another person asked him that same question again, he was going to explode. "I care for this woman. I genuinely care for her in a way I didn't care for Olivia at the end. I don't know why I feel this way about her, but I can assure you that nothing has happened between us. For all I know she probably hates my guts and never wants to see me again. And I don't blame her. Do you know why? Because she's done nothing wrong, because she's had to stand by and listen to you all talk about her as if she wasn't good enough to sit at this table. I'll tell you one thing, she is more fitting to sit at this table than Olivia ever was, and if you ever go to know her—if she ever gives me a chance to fix things—you'd say the same."

His parents stared at him open-mouthed.

"Oh, Reed," his mother said softly. "You seem so smitten by her."

"Been bitten by a bug, I'd say," his father added, grumpily. "We're going home, Alison."

"We are?"

"Already?" Reed asked, and yet he wasn't against the idea. They needed space. And two thousand miles was a good enough distance between them.

"This has been too much for your mother to take in."

"I'm not sure that's true, Wilbur," his mother replied, testily.

But clearly, it made sense for all of them to get back to normality. Things were going to get busy once news of the announcement spread, and he still had to cancel all things related to the wedding. There was no way he would leave it to Olivia to handle that.

"If you're sure," he said to his parents.

"We're sure," his father said.

"I think it's best if we let everything settle down," his mother said.

He couldn't agree more.

# CHAPTER 32

After his parents left the next morning, Reed buried himself in his study for the rest of the day.

When Jenna still didn't turn up to work, he called, but her cell phone was switched off, and he didn't want to call the agency in fear that it might land her in trouble. He'd already decided to pay her a visit once he'd cleared away his backlog of work.

"Your favorite," said Cecile, placing a plate of southern fried chicken in front of him at lunchtime. "I know how much you love this." The sight of it perked him up. "Thanks, Cecile."

"Is that all the enthusiasm you can muster?"

He forced a huge smile. "Thanks, Cecile. I appreciate it immensely."

"You've been looking miserable for days, and I don't blame you. Been a lot to take in."

"I can imagine, especially for you, walking back into this."

"I was thinking more about you."

He groaned, not wanting to talk about it. The past few days had taken a mental toll, but he was worried about Jenna, and trying to work out what to do. This morning he'd been busy dealing with urgent business matters, and he had yet to deal with the condo in Forest Heights which he hoped Olivia had vacated.

"Things always work out for the best in the long-term," Cecile said, patting his hand. She had never liked Olivia, she'd never said it out loud, but he could tell, and he was certain Olivia had picked up on this, too.

"Let's hope," he replied, picking up another chicken drumstick.

"Aren't you glad you escaped?" asked Cecile, not one to hold back. "Imagine if you had gone on and married her." And when he didn't reply, she said, "I see. I see what you're so moody about. I like her."

He bit into the chicken, and savored the fried, smoky-flavored taste, loved the crunch of the fried breadcrumbs. "Who?"

"You know full well who."

"It's a mess right now," he said, licking his fingers.

"It's not going to sort itself out if you're going to sit there eating fried chicken all day long."

"I'm thinking," he told her, chewing slowly.

"Whatever you're thinking, make it quick. That girl is hurting, as anyone would be hurting if they'd had to listen to the sort of things she had to. You should be over there making things better for her, not sitting here feeling sorry for yourself while devouring a plate of fried chicken."

"You're the one who put that plate in front of me!"

Cecile winked at him.

"I was waiting for my parents to leave before I talked to Jenna" he said. "I know her. She can't be bought, or wined and dined. It's not so easy with her."

"Maybe she doesn't want to be wined and dined. Maybe all she wants is a bit of respect?"

～

It was all over social media like a rash. It was Shay who had alerted her, after her boss, Francine, had had a meeting with Shay to ask about the rumors. As a result of which they had decided that Jenna should lay low until Reed Knight himself commented on the situation.

Apparently, Olivia had posted in her numerous social media accounts about her broken engagement. She had hinted at an affair. Though she had been clever not to mention names, she had suggested that there was a third-party involved in the break-up. Somehow, through her network of friends, and the rumor mill that was rampant in Starling Bay, the news had spread like a tsunami within a few days.

It wasn't long before the blame was pinned on 'the maid' at the Knight Mansion.

So, taking on board Shay's boss's advice, Jenna had refrained from working at the Knight mansion 'until further notice.'

The manager at the preschool had also called the agency telling them that they no longer wanted Jenna to work for them.

She was devastated, but felt even more gutted for Shay. Her friend had done her best to get her work, and now she was getting in trouble with her boss for it, when it was clearly not Shay's fault.

While it wasn't Jenna's fault either, she would have happily taken the hit for it.

It shocked Jenna that the preschool had turned against her. Nobody would have seen her coming to work at that time of the morning. Nobody would have even known who she was but the fact that someone had gone to the trouble of having her removed from employment there told her that it was only a matter of time before the entire town would be up in arms against her. Clearly, people she did not know, blamed her for breaking up Olivia and Reed.

The injustice of the whole situation ate away at her. She was sure that in time, Reed would walk away unscathed, and Olivia would emerge as a martyr. Only her name would be dragged through the mud.

Worse, she hadn't heard from Reed. By now at least she had expected a phone call, or a text, if not that first day, then the next, but when he hadn't gotten in touch a few days later, she turned her phone off and hardened herself to the fact that he didn't care. It was enough to make her want to curl up into a ball and stay in bed, except that this wasn't her bed, either.

She was only lying here because Shay was watching TV and Jenna wanted to be alone. She felt bad, as if she had ruined things for Shay, and tried to give her friend some space. This wasn't even her apartment, nothing here belonged to her, not even the sofa she slept on every night.

She had started to consider the possibility of quitting altogether and heading back to Chicago again. Compared to hanging around here, Chicago didn't look so bad anymore.

There was also the matter of Reed Knight. Staying away from him seemed to be the more sensible option. He had been trouble for her before, and he was trouble now.

She'd fallen for his sweet talk; she saw that now, for sweet talking was all it had been. When things had turned bad with Olivia, Reed had turned his attentions to Jenna simply because he could.

It had been days since he'd kissed her on the nose, and whispered those endearments that had her thinking she was special.

It was nothing, she told herself; a peck on the nose, holding hands, sweet talking. It was all wrapped up in thoughts and feelings and bow-tied with longing, but she had meant nothing to him. Reed's words had been empty ones.

He'd had a chance to prove himself, to stand up for her in front of his parents, but he'd said and done nothing.

At the sound of a knock on the door, she started to wonder why Shay was knocking on her own door. But then it opened and Shay's head popped around the corner. "There's someone here to see you," she said, looking oddly flushed.

Before Jenna even had a chance to sit up properly and adjust her tank top, Reed walked in.

Goosebumps stood to attention all over her bare arms. "What are you doing here?" she asked, slightly shocked and slightly angry, and not in the mood to see him.

"That's a fine welcome."

"But seriously," she asked, hastily smoothing down her hair, and pulling up the shoulder strap which had fallen down. "What are you doing here *now?*" She hoped he caught the inflection in her tone.

He did. "I wanted to come earlier," he replied carefully. "I called you but your phone was switched off."

"It was switched on for the first two days."

"It's not been easy having my parents around," he said, sighing heavily. "I wanted to come sooner. I should have called you sooner. I'm sorry I didn't. I didn't know which fire to fight first."

She had assumed he'd had a lot to deal with, and she had tried to understand his shortcomings with regards to that, but he'd left her to deal with things alone. If she'd been looking for a signal from him that she mattered, he'd failed miserably.

Climbing off the bed, she slipped on her sweatshirt, preferring some body armor when dealing with him. It wasn't that Reed invaded her space too much, just that when faced with those smoldering blue eyes, and that soft, husky voice, her defenses weakened.

"Cold?" he asked, keeping his distance and hovering by the wall.

"I wasn't expecting any visitors." She stood up and pulled her hair out of her sweatshirt. "How are your parents?"

"Why?" He looked slightly surprised.

"Because they're your parents, and they matter to you." She sensed that their opinions mattered to him.

"They went back this morning."

"They've left already?"

"They couldn't take the shock."

"It figures," she said, folding her arms. They were probably more shocked that Reed was caught with her, than they would have been at Olivia's behavior. Jenna would bet her job on it, which was saying something because she only had one job left.

"It's not just about you, Jenna. They were shocked about the engagement and everything."

"Mostly the 'everything'," she air-quoted. Which reminded her of something she needed to say. "Thanks for sticking up for me that day." Her voice was hard and prickly, like barbed wire.

He walked closer, walked around the side of the bed so that he was about an arm's width away from her.

"I'm sorry. I should have come after you when you left, but I wasn't prepared for everything that had happened. It was one thing after another, and my parents turning up unexpectedly completely threw me."

"Do you have any idea how it felt, having your parents look at me as if I was nothing?"

"I know, and I'm sorry. I feel real bad about that. I wish I'd said something, but defending you at that moment would have made the situation worse, Jenna. They didn't know the engagement was off when they saw us together. It was an added shock."

"Olivia had called them to come over here but hadn't told them?"

"My fiancée is very clever, very sly."

"She is." She could imagine how awkward it must have been for him to deal with that entire situation, but she wasn't going to give in easily. He stared at her, sending a shiver across her body. The room wasn't that cold, but having Reed's gaze pinned to hers made her body react. She rubbed her arms.

"Doesn't Shay turn the heat on?"

"She does, sometimes. It costs." And even though she was able to contribute towards the rent now, she wasn't going to tell Shay to do that when it wasn't her apartment.

"I meant to come earlier but I got tied up cancelling wedding stuff."

"Hmmm." He looked uncomfortable, but she didn't feel up to making him feel welcome.

"I shouldn't have imposed and shown up in your room like this."

"It isn't my room. It's Shay's. I sleep on the couch."

"You sleep on the couch?" he asked, his jaw twitching.

"I can't afford my own apartment yet."

"Ah, that's right. So you said, that's why you had to take on those other jobs."

"I've lost both of the other jobs. Well, sort of. The preschool told me not to come anymore and—"

"They did what?" He looked astonished.

"They didn't want me. They called Francine specifically and told her."

"Francine?"

"Shay's boss at the agency."

"Damn, news spreads so fast in a place like this," he muttered, his face hardening. "I'm sorry they did that."

"And Francine found out about the 'other woman' responsible for your breakup, and told me to stay put until they heard from you."

"What?" he looked at her in disbelief. "I assumed you didn't come because of my parents, and because I've been an asshole to you, and for everything that's happened, with Olivia, and Pennington, and the watch. I thought you needed more time, and that's why you stayed away."

"I didn't want to be there while your parents were, but I need to work, and I need to earn, so," she shrugged, "I would have come if not yesterday, then today. I had planned to return to your place, but Francine suggested I wait it out a while."

He swiped a hand across his face as if he was unable to comprehend the scale of things. "This all happened in a matter of days?"

She gave a mirthless laugh. "You've probably been stuck in your study the whole time, oblivious to the news."

Reed slapped a hand to the back of his neck. "Pennington mentioned something about the agency," he said, his voice trailing off as he connected the dots. "I've been so busy, I didn't get around to calling them back."

"Meanwhile, the rest of us who live in the real world, get to deal with real world consequences."

It sounded bitter, said like that. But once again it seemed unjust. Reed could afford to shut himself off, and not suffer any consequences. She'd had to deal with the fallout of a situation which hadn't even been hers in the making.

"I'll call her tonight and explain. I'll tell her that you're completely innocent, and you didn't break us up. I'll make her see reason."

He could make one person see reason, but could he change the viewpoint of the entire town?

It had caught her by surprise, the speed with which the news had spread. She hadn't expected Olivia's social profile to go viral so instantly. But then Shay told her that Olivia had accounts on all the social media platforms, and there was already extra interest in the town about her because of the photoshoot, added to which, Olivia was engaged to Reed Knight, which made for more frenzy.

If there had been no photoshoot, no high-profile magazine, and no high-society engagement, nobody would have given a hoot what happened to Olivia.

It explained everything.

Reed had ventured out to see her. It gave her some solace, but she steeled herself against forgiving him so quickly. "I'm probably known as the woman who had an affair with Reed Knight and caused his engagement to break up."

"That's a crock of lies," he said, his temper rising. "I'm going to fix that."

"It's not your fault. Your ex-fiancée spreading her woe-is-me story on social media isn't helping. She's making me out to be the reason you split." She sat down on the bed, because it was awkward standing facing him.

"Looks like I'm going to have to get in touch with my lawyer."

"Why, are you going to sue her?"

"Tell her to behave herself or else."

He followed suit and sat down a distance away from her. It felt strange having him be so near, here at Shay's place, outside of their normal environment. It was starting to feel oddly comfortable, when the last thing she should have felt was comfortable, given all that had gone on.

A part of her wondered if he would reach out and touch her, and a part of her waited in anticipation.

"I'm sorry my parents behaved the way they did. I'm sorry about Pennington too. Actually, *he's* sorry."

"He is?"

"Once I'd explained to him what Olivia was like, and what a saint you were in comparison, he saw that he'd jumped to the wrong conclusion too quickly."

She considered that for a moment, the image of the tall, thin, hard-edged Pennington feeling bad about the way he'd treated her. It was hard to believe. "How's he doing post-Olivia?"

"He's perfectly fine. He was wondering when you would return to work."

"Depends on when you speak to Shay's boss," she reminded him.

"Do you want to come back?"

"Why?" she asked, wondering what had prompted this question. Had his parents threatened to disown him if she set foot in the house again? Up until he had walked through the door tonight she'd been tempted to find other work, through another agency if need be. And she had also been looking at online courses so that she could train in other lines of work.

"Because I need you."

That was hardly an answer. She shivered, and prayed that he hadn't sensed it, because she wasn't shivering due to the cold. This man—like the boy many years ago—for whom she had started to feel an attraction, had an effect on her which wasn't going to end well. Whether she gave in or not, she was doomed. Doomed if she gave in to the desire which started up each time she was within a few yards of him, and doomed if she tried to ignore it and go about her daily work.

How could she still work for Reed, feeling the way she did? "I can imagine the dust must have started to pile up," she retorted.

"I need *you*, Jenna. I don't need a maid. I can always get another one of those."

"And this time a proper one with real experience and references. Shay told me Pennington had asked to see my resume a few weeks ago."

"He's loyal to me, and to the family, and back then he was team Olivia. He's not so bad, if you give him half a chance. It's up to you if you want to come back, but I understand if you don't. I won't like it, but I'll understand."

She wasn't sure now. Couldn't make head or tail of what would happen between them after all that she had seen and heard. "Your parents hate me, don't they?"

"*I* like you. I thought we felt the same about one another." He reached out to place his hand on her arm, but sensing her coldness, pulled it away. Once again, that wasn't the answer she'd been hoping for. The fact that he hadn't offered any further insight into what his parents had said about her, made her think the worst.

It made her realize, even if she dared to believe that Reed was interested in her, that she would only ever be a maid in their eyes. Nothing good could ever come of being with Reed.

"What's wrong? I know I let you down, Jenna, and I'm sorry, but I came as soon as I could. I wanted to see that you were okay."

"I *am* okay." Maybe not one hundred percent, but she was going to be okay. She had already made up her mind about it.

He stood up, sensing her aloofness. "I'll call Shay's boss tonight and smooth over everything."

She sat up. "I'm not sure I want to come back."

"What?"

"I'm not sure it would work out."

His jaw twitched as he contemplated her reply. "But you need the money."

"I'll find another job."

"You've already lost the preschool."

She swallowed. "I'll figure something out. I'm not even sure that Starling Bay is the right place for me."

Surprise flickered across his face. "What's brought this on?"

*You, and this, and everything you haven't said.*

"I've been thinking. I'm not stupid, I have a brain, and I think I should try to get some office jobs."

His face brightened. "I couldn't agree more. I totally understand you not wanting to work as a maid"

"I don't think it's a good idea for me to be around you, either. Like I've always said to you, you could get away with things and still have people look up to you. I'll always have this stigma."

"Of what, exactly?"

"Of being the one who split you and your fiancée up, and of being a maid at that," she replied, hinting at the way his parents had spoken about her that day.

"You have to ignore what my parents said."

"I can't. They made it perfectly clear what they thought of me."

"It was a shock to them."

"And what they said was a shock to me."

"I'm sorry, for them, and on behalf of them."

"It doesn't mean a thing. It doesn't change a thing, either. You are Reed Knight, and they expect great things from you."

"That doesn't mean anything."

"Everything in your life comes so easily for you, Reed."

"I don't even know what you're trying to say."

"That's because we don't speak the same language."

He scratched his jaw. "You're trying to push me away."

"I don't think anything good will come out of us trying to be together."

He frowned. "You can't give up on us so easily."

"There is no us, Reed. Who are we kidding?"

"Is that your decision?" He shrugged and looked as if he was going to laugh, or mock her, but didn't. "You're deciding we have no future when we haven't even tried."

"If you stood where I'm standing, and saw things from my point of view, you wouldn't even go there."

"But I'm seeing it from mine, Jenna, and I know we can."

"That's the difference between us, don't you see. We're the haves and have-nots, you and I, and we each know our place."

He shook his head. "You had more fire in you when you were a maid."

She huffed out a gasp, because his words had been like a slap in her face.

"You've given up, just like that. You heard my parents say things, and it killed your spark."

"It would have killed yours had our roles been reversed."

"I can't change who I am, but I am not who you think I am." He looked hurt as he said it, crushed even. Then he walked out, leaving her feeling hurt and sad.

# CHAPTER 33

The phones hadn't stopped ringing.

News about the broken engagement suddenly mushroomed, and while Pennington and Cecile fielded the calls as best as they could, even so, things were full-on crazy.

When it came to his friends and business associates, Reed attempted quick, right-to-the-point conversations, knowing that if he didn't speak now, and set the record straight, his reluctance would be taken as a sign of his guilt. He was eager to dispel rumors about a third party being involved in the split.

He'd spoken to Francine at the agency earlier and she had assured him that Jenna still had the office cleaning contract, and there might possibly be a few other jobs in the pipeline.

That had made him feel slightly upbeat, compared to how he had felt when he'd gone to see Jenna a few days ago. He hadn't expected her to welcome him with open arms, but he hadn't expected her to push him away.

Having had time to think things over, he understood. She was hurt. She'd already had bad memories of him, and his wealthy background. These things had become super magnified with his parents' arrival.

He could have done more, but he hadn't, and now she believed they had no chance of a future together.

She had given up.

But he wasn't ready to.

Of course, he had experienced people whispering behind his back, but it was always behind his back. He'd give them the middle finger if they had the guts to say something to his face, but cowards and gossips never did.

After the initial madness started to die down, he met with Dylan and Rourke. His friends had already threatened to turn up on his doorstep if he didn't meet them face-to-face and tell them what had been going on.

"Jenna Lawson?" asked Rourke, for what must have been the third or fourth time.

"Quit hounding him," Dylan said.

"Sorry pal, but this is big news. I couldn't believe it when the girls at work told me. News gets around. Come to mention it, why did I have to hear it from the girls at work? How come you didn't—"

"Will you quit it?" Dylan snapped. "He didn't tell us straightaway because I assume he had a lot going on. Right?" Dylan asked, turning to Reed. "If you don't want to talk about it, we don't have to."

"We *should* talk about it," said Rourke. "Because that's why he wanted to meet us, and it helps to talk, that's what women say." Reed let them carry on like two ten-year olds, talking about him as if he wasn't there.

"What's gotten into you?" Dylan said to Rourke. "Did you get extra shots of caffeine on your way here?"

"I didn't get a chance to pass by the bookshop today. But seriously guys, come on," Rourke looked at them, "this is *big* news. *Huge. I'm* surprised. Aren't you? *Shocked* would be a better word."

"Silence would be even better," Dylan muttered.

"It's a shock, I get it," said Reed. He lowered his head, wanting to drown out the noise. He'd been looking forward to seeing his friends. Had needed the distraction. Needed to talk it out with someone. Maybe he should have called Dylan and arranged to meet him first.

As it was, he'd debated about coming to the Blue Velvet Bar. He'd wanted to go somewhere less busy. But, he reasoned, if Jenna could go out to work and confront people, then he shouldn't shy away either.

"How are you doing?" Dylan asked him again.

"I'm getting busy with the old movie theater. That's the main focus lately."

"Good. Keeping busy helps."

"So, *did* you have an affair?" Rourke asked. Dylan's head turned to his right, so that Reed couldn't read his expression, but he imagined that Rourke was at the receiving end of a death stare about now.

"Why are you so interested?" he asked.

"Because this is so out of the blue. I didn't see it coming. I mean, the way you both were at the ball and all."

Reed almost choked at that and wondered what Rourke had seen. Of course, the guy had been busy talking to Jenna at every opportunity, so he probably hadn't been paying much attention to things.

"Merry didn't believe it at first either," said Dylan.

"And you?" Reed asked him.

His friend made a face as if he didn't want to answer. "If I was to be honest, I wasn't surprised."

That's what he'd thought. Dylan with his super-sleuth skills had likely realized a while back. "Did you and Olivia part on amicable terms?"

"Not really."

His friends looked at one another. He picked up his whisky glass and swirled the amber colored liquid around. He hadn't mentioned the other dramas, nothing about the watch, or his parents catching him and Jenna in what looked like a compromising situation.

"This must be hard on Jenna," Dylan offered.

"It is."

"I feel sorry for her," Rourke added. "News spreads fast in Starling Bay. Doesn't help that Olivia's so famous."

"She's only famous because of Reed," Dylan pointed out.

Reed's shoulders tensed. "Didn't help either that she made those nasty comments about Jenna. They're completely untrue, by the way. I wasn't having an affair, and Jenna and I weren't up to anything. You both know me, right? You know I'd never do anything like that." But he liked her. Cared for her. Had feelings for her.

A group of business associates walked in, nodded their heads at him, then sat down at one of the tables further away. Usually people stopped to talk to him, but tonight they seemed to be giving him a wide berth. He was glad.

They were silent again, until Dylan spoke up. "We're here for you, anytime you need to talk."

"I know."

"So, does Jenna still clean for you?" Rourke asked.

"No," he replied gruffly. "What's the fascination with Jenna?"

"I'm interested," Rourke exclaimed. "Clearly, *you're* okay, but Jenna's seen as an outsider right now. It must be hard."

"It is." Reed lifted the whiskey glass to his lips. "I just wish I'd stuck up for her more when my parents were being obnoxious."

"Your mom, too?" Dylan asked, surprised.

"She was caught off guard." Reed imagined it would have been like a kick to the stomach, his parents seeing him and Jenna looking as if they were about to kiss, when they had no idea about the engagement.

"Ouch," said Rourke. "I can imagine your dad being opinionated."

"You know my dad."

"But ultimately, your parents will want you to be happy," remarked Dylan. "Most parents do."

"Most parents," Reed muttered.

"It depends on what happens, right?" Rourke asked. "With you and Jenna. I mean, do you *like* her, and if so, when did that happen? Because you were with…Olivia, so…. And does Jenna feel the same way about you? Did anything happen?"

Dylan cleared his throat, with a little too much exaggeration.

"But we don't have to talk about that now," Rourke added, hastily.

"No, we don't," Dylan said.

"I don't know what happens now." Reed ignored the machine-gun round of questions. He wasn't sure what happened now, between them. Ever since he'd left Jenna, he hadn't called her, or seen her. Cecile had asked about her, and so had Pennington. So had his mother, when she'd called yesterday, but he had no news for her, other than to say Jenna no longer worked for him. He'd also told her that everything wedding-wise had been cancelled, and that Olivia was back in The Hamptons.

He wondered if she had a backup fiancé-in-waiting there. He had his doubts about the photographer now because Olivia wasn't the type to be interested in anyone except the man at the top. She aimed high; it was a self-preservation tactic.

Jenna was so different. She had been trying to make her way in life by herself, and the odds had been stacked against her.

Maybe he could pull a few strings, seeing that he and his family had been the source of so much pain for her.

∼

They were having dinner at Roxy's Diner.

"I don't think that's a good idea," Shay said. "You don't need to go to another agency out of town. Francine believes you had nothing to do with the split. Reed called and spoke to her. In time, most people will realize that Olivia was being spiteful."

"It's a small town. Reed Knight is a big fish here. I don't stand a chance. People's prejudices are hard to shift."

Shay had been good to her, but Jenna still felt bad that her boss had had to get involved, and they'd lost the preschool contract.

This morning, after her office cleaning shift, she had gone out of town and signed up at other recruitment agencies with the aim of finding work away from Starling Bay. To her surprise, Shay wasn't on board with the idea at all.

"But Reed has spoken up for you. Are you still not going to give him a chance?"

Jenna shook her head. She'd told Shay about the conversation with Reed that night, and about everything that had ever happened between them before; it wasn't much in the way of anything physical, so she hadn't expected Shay to understand. But her friend had found their conversations, and their few snatched moments utterly romantic, and had told her so. "He's a real gentleman."

"If he was a real gentleman, he'd have stood up for me when his parents were looking down at me."

"Sounds to me as if he tried to do what he could," countered Shay. "If he liked you, if he showed you in those subtle ways how he feels, and if you feel the same, why not go for it?"

"You don't know what it's like, feeling as if you're not good enough."

"Does Reed make you feel like that?" Shay asked.

It was a question she didn't answer, because he didn't.

"You should give him a chance, Jenna, and you should give yourself a break."

"A break?"

"You are *enough,* Jenna. Stop thinking of yourself as someone less than him. You have to let it go, this whole rich man, poor maid scenario."

"It's not a scenario, it's the story of my life."

Shay threw her hands into the air. "Then, like I told you before, re-write it."

"It's not that simple, being attracted to someone when you know there is no future, no chance of anything happening because of who he is."

"If there's no chance of anything happening, then why did Reed Knight come over to see you the other day, and why did he take the time to call Francine and explain everything?"

Jenna dipped an onion ring into her ketchup. She didn't know. She was scared to hope, to think that the feelings he had shown might be real after all, scared to think that something *could* come of it. "I've got three more weeks of the online accounting course, and then I can take the test," she replied, focusing on the thing she could control the outcome of.

"Great, but you're avoiding the question."

"I know. I'm trying to re-write the story of my life, and I'm focusing on my career." She bit into her onion ring and smiled.

"You can have both, a career and let someone into your life, who cares about you," said Shay, talking like an agony-aunt.

"Because you have both, don't you?" Jenna asked, throwing the ball back in her friend's court.

Shay narrowed her eyes at her.

"Hopefully I'll get a good office job out of town," Jenna continued.

"Francine believes you. She's trying real hard to find you some work here."

"She's been looking for a week now. People don't want me. My mistake was to come and settle in a small town where everyone knows everyone's business."

"What happened to your fighting spirit?" Shay asked. "Did the Knights extinguish it?"

"No."

"Are you sure?"

She sat up and picked out another onion ring. Yes, she was sure. She had been thinking about Reed lately, but she didn't know what to do. She also hadn't liked the idea of leaving the Knight mansion abruptly without saying a proper goodbye to Cecile.

"I'll go and see him when I have a job," she said.

"That's something," Shay threw back, her voice heavy on the sarcasm.

# CHAPTER 34

He couldn't protect Jenna from the wrath of the townspeople, but he knew someone who could; a woman whom many in Starling Bay feared and avoided. A woman who could be the perfect wing woman for Jenna.

"What brings you here young man, at such a busy time?" Hyacinth Fitzsimmons smiled at him and he couldn't help but stare at her overzealous application of bright pink lipstick. It had run onto two of her teeth and distracted him. He wanted to tell her, but couldn't yet bring himself to.

"I need your help, Hyacinth." He sat across from her, at the wooden desk in her office at the Town Hall building.

"*My* help?" Hyacinth clasped her hands together and eyed him carefully. He was certain that she'd had heard the rumors by now.

"I can't think of anyone else who can help."

"I will gladly do what I can. How are things with you, Reed?"

"As well as they could be."

They stared at one another for an awkward few seconds. "Your parents returned to Montana rather quickly."

"Yes. They were sad to have to cancel your dinner date."

"I was looking forward to seeing them, but…" Her expression

turned somber, and she bobbed her head, as if weighing up what to say. "It's understandable, given the circumstances."

"Yes."

"I was sorry to hear that you had called off the wedding."

"These things happen."

"Your fiancée was such a lovely young lady."

He forced himself to stifle the loud exhale. "Olivia *is* a lovely young lady, and I'm sure she'll make some lovely young man extremely happy. Unfortunately, it won't be me."

Hyacinth's eyebrows lifted, and she waited for him to elaborate.

"Just so that we're clear, there was no one else involved in our break-up," he said, shifting his position and sitting up taller. He placed his arms on the armrest. "I know *you* don't like to gossip, but you know how most people do."

She fell for the lie. "Yes, yes, I know. Terrible. Terrible thing for people to judge."

"And judge they do."

"Disgusting."

"Without knowing the truth."

"Absolutely."

They smiled at one another again.

"So." Hyacinth rubbed her hands together. "What is it that you think I can help you with?"

And so the sweetening commenced. "I know how much my family look up to you, Hyacinth. Both our families go back a long way in this town. We know the code, we know how important reputation is," he said, nodding. Hyacinth mirrored his pose, her eyes suggesting she was hanging onto his every word. "You know my family, and you know my father's code of ethics, and you know me. I hope you understand that I would never do anything improper."

"Yes, yes, of course."

"And I know how well respected you are, Hyacinth, here in this town. You are the pillar of the community, and a person that many of us look up to."

She smiled at him, baring her lipsticked-teeth, obviously rapt with his assessment of her. He glanced down at his lap, and looked at the time on his watch. "This is a delicate situation, and…" he looked up, adopting a stern expression. "I can't think of anyone better suited to this than you."

"Me?"

"Yes, you, Hyacinth. People love you…"

"Oh," she said, suddenly turning coquettish. "I don't know about that."

"They do. They admire your strength and your sense of fairness."

"Well, thank you, Reed. But what is it that you want me to do?"

"I know in the past you've had openings for someone to help out in your office." The Town Hall always had requirements for extra admin help throughout the year, but not many people applied. Not many people relished the idea of working alongside Hyacinth.

"We always need someone to help out. The Town Hall is such a central part of town life, as you know and there is so much administrative work to do."

"That's what I thought. Jenna Lawson is looking for work, and having someone like you take her under your wing for a few months would be a great help to her, I'm sure."

"Jenna Lawson?"

"The maid who used to work for me."

Hyacinth's mouth fell open. "Take her under my wing?"

He cleared his throat. "Of course, you understand there was no impropriety. She wasn't responsible for anything to do with me calling off the wedding, but sometimes people can be cruel and rumors will circulate. It's been unfortunate that Jenna was caught up in it".

Hyacinth looked shocked, as if he'd thrown a jug of water over her.

"You're not one of those people," he continued, "and I know you'll want to make sure that all the citizens in this town are dealt with fairly." He leaned forward. "If you took Jenna Lawson under your wing, if you perhaps offered her a job here, if I perhaps introduced you to the owner of a certain agency so that you could work out a deal that suited you, you would be helping Jenna out. You understand how the townspeople seem to have turned against her?"

"Are you asking me to cover for you, Reed?"

He exhaled slowly. Pretty in garish pink she might be, but Hyacinth was no fool. "Jenna Lawson has been unfairly treated."

"That's what happens if you break up a couple. Of course," she cleared her throat. "It takes two to tango."

"Except that nobody was doing the tango, Hyacinth. I can assure you of that."

She pinned her gaze on him, and he could see the cogs turning inside that busy brain of hers. "I hear you're renovating the old movie theater."

And there it was. "We are. The project starts in the next few weeks."

"The Fitzsimmons Theater has a lovely ring to it, don't you think?"

Surely she wasn't proposing that he named the old movie theater after her family name as well? "You think the movie theater could benefit in such a way?"

"We are from old stock, Reed, you and I. It's good to keep the family names running. Starling Bay is better for it."

He didn't agree, but he forced himself to on this occasion.

"We understand one another perfectly, Hyacinth. I'll see what I can do, but Jenna mustn't know."

Hyacinth raised a leathery eyebrow. A flash of questioning zoomed across her features, but she managed not to ask any questions. "I'll see to it that she never finds out."

"I'll arrange it with the recruitment agency."

"There's no need to go through an agency—"

"Jenna can't know I was trying to help her."

"Should I ask why you are?"

"Because she wasn't born with everything stacked in her favor, and she's lost a work contract because of the rumors. It's not her fault. So, do we have a deal?"

"Yes."

He stood up and held out his hand.

"You surprise me, Reed, but in a good way. I can't say that about many people." Hyacinth shook his hand and smiled again.

"Thank you," he said. "Oh, and you have a lipstick stain on your teeth."

# CHAPTER 35

It had come out of the blue, and it seemed almost freakily serendipitous. She couldn't believe it when Shay told her.

"The old dragon has advertised for some help with the administration at the Town Hall." Shay told her, as they sat down to eat the dinner which Jenna had prepared.

"Which old dragon?" asked Jenna, picking up her cutlery.

"Hyacinth Fitzsimmons."

"She's still here?" Jenna remembered the woman as clear as day. She was hard to miss. "Does she still wear bright blush and lipstick?"

Shay made a face. "She does, with her being a lot older now, it looks garish. She looks like a drag queen."

"Did she ever get married?"

"No, not as far as I know, but pay attention, Jenna. This job is at the Town Hall, and it pays well. Francine said to mention it to you because it sounded ideal."

"For me?" Jenna frowned. "I don't think anyone in their right minds would want to work alongside Hyacinth."

"But it would pay well, and it would be here, and you

wouldn't have to commute out of town each day. And, working for her would be a sign to everyone that you are innocent."

"Of what?"

"In that whole Olivia saga."

"How's that?"

"You'll be working for Hyacinth. She wouldn't hire anyone who had a whiff of notoriety about them."

"I do need the work," said Jenna, pensively.

"Francine really wants to put you forward for the position, and it would be an office job which is exactly what you wanted. Think about it, Jenna. You could give up the cleaning job."

"I'd *have* to give that up." She couldn't do that and then spend a whole day at work after.

"Okay, so now, the best bit. Francine said I could tell you; it's paying double what you got as a maid at the Knight mansion."

"Double?" A virtual cash register caching'd in Jenna's head. She did the calculations. If she took this on, she'd be able to move out in a month or so and rent an apartment of her own. "Why is Francine so eager to put me forward for it? I don't have proper qualifications for office work yet."

"I told her you're doing the online accounting course and you're doing the test soon. Plus, she feels bad for you, getting the rough end of the deal."

She felt suddenly happier. Lighter, and happier; something she hadn't felt in weeks. "I'll come and see her about it tomorrow morning first thing."

"Talking of being a maid at the Knight mansion," said Shay, "They've taken on a new hire."

Jenna stopped cutting in to her fishcake. "A new maid?"

"She's in her late forties."

Jenna smiled. "Cecile will be pleased. I might go and see her one day."

"Only Cecile?"

"I might go and say goodbye to Mr. Knight as well."

He took the call in the library, which was where he preferred to work lately because his study seemed too claustrophobic these days.

"You can go to press, but the story is a lie, and I'm sure your readers won't like being duped."

Reed hung up. They were starting to get scared enough for the CEO of the fashion magazine to call him. The people behind the photoshoot needed to know the truth. Reed's lawyers had contacted them weeks ago, threatening to sue if the magazine went ahead and published that feature. But up until now, they'd obviously thought he was bluffing.

What might also have prompted this phone call was that he had done something he never thought he'd do, and he'd done it only because he wanted to clear Jenna's name; he'd given an interview to the Starling Bay Daily. It was a small newspaper, a dot in the ocean compared to the reach and distribution of the fashion magazine, but he hoped it would throw an extra obstacle in their path.

The Starling Bay Daily interview had been short, but he hoped, had done enough for damage control and, more importantly, would do enough to clear Jenna's name.

Maybe the fashion company would go ahead and print their feature anyway, but who would want to print something that was clearly fake news? His and Olivia's fabricated domestic bliss had been a complete lie.

He was trying to keep his head down and get on with things, but people were still calling to ask if the news was true, and he was still taking those types of phone calls. His parents were coming to terms with things. His mother had understood why he had broken off the engagement, but it was still going to take some time as far as his father was concerned. As far the situation with Jenna, his parents hadn't asked, and even if they had, he had nothing to tell them.

It had been weeks since he'd spoken to Jenna, and some days he wasn't sure what to do about it. Whether to call her, or go and see her.

Francine had told him that she'd come over a few days ago and had signed the contract to work at the Town Hall.

That had been good news.

And the new maid had settled into her job and was getting on with things. He was trying to do the same, only, he couldn't.

Jenna Lawson was hard to forget, and not just because of her blue-tipped hair.

# CHAPTER 36

She braced herself. She'd come back to return the bike, and to see Cecile and say a proper goodbye. But Reed was also behind these doors, and she wasn't sure how she was going to deal with seeing him. Her rocketing heartbeat told her it wasn't going to be easy.

She still had the key to the front-door, but decided to ring the doorbell instead of letting herself in and scaring the heck out of everyone. Pennington answered. "Jenna!" he exclaimed, looking dumbstruck. "This is a surprise."

"I've returned the bike, it's over by the wall, so please don't go calling the cops on me."

He opened his mouth to say something, but Cecile had already bulldozed her way in front of him. "Jenna!" she cried, holding out her arms. "Welcome back."

Cecile's arms wrapped around her and Jenna felt a surge of warm comfort. "Hi," she said, when Cecile finally pulled away and let her breathe. "You left without a word." The cook pointed an accusing finger at her.

"I had no choice," replied Jenna. She looked over at the kitchen all the way at the other end of the hallway.

"Come in." Cecile herded her in.

"I haven't got all day," Jenna began.

"Got a few hours?" Cecile asked, and started walking towards the kitchen. Jenna followed.

"A couple." She looked around as she passed the familiar door of Reed's study, wondering if he would be in there, and if he'd heard her voice.

"I'm so glad to see you again, Jenna," said Pennington.

"Let me have her to myself for a while," Cecile said crossly, "You can ask her for forgiveness when I'm done."

"I heard you have a new maid," said Jenna, slightly disappointed that Reed wasn't in the kitchen. She started to wonder if he was even here at all.

"She's not you, but she's good enough. You and I didn't have enough time to get to know one another, Jenna, but I feel bad for all the crazy stuff you've had to go through. Reed told me about you losing your other job, and that you'd decided not to come back here."

"He told you?"

"It wasn't right. Wasn't right at all for his folks to be carrying on like they did. But Reed's got a good heart on him."

Jenna shrugged, and looked away, then caught sight of something on the countertop. "Olive sandwich rolls."

"He asked me to make them. Said they had to be olive," said Cecile, making a low disapproving noise in her throat. "Told me he didn't want hot lunches anymore."

"He did like them," said Jenna, remembering all those times when she had felt sorry for him and had made his snacks.

"I don't know what voodoo you've done on that man, but… well, he's been moping around like a wounded soldier most days."

"A wounded soldier?"

"Keeps himself locked away in the library, says he can't bear to be in the study much."

This didn't sound like the man she knew. Even if he was hurt, he'd try and hide it. "Reed?"

"Yes, him. You know how his parents drain that boy's spirits dry."

Having met his parents, Jenna could see that Cecile had a point.

"What happened to your hair?"

"I decided that it was time to look professional."

"Wasn't nothing wrong with you before," snorted Cecile. "I liked those blue ends. Gave you character."

"I'm working alongside Hyacinth Fitzsimmons," she announced proudly. "Got myself a job at the Town Hall. Time for a new start, and a new look."

Cecile's eyes widened to saucers. "Hyacinth Fitzsimmons? You might as well go for a walk on a bed of hot coals, girl."

Jenna giggled. They talked for a while, and she told Cecile more about the new job which she was due to start next week. She couldn't say no when Cecile pushed a plate of lemon muffins towards her. They talked some more, and she had a second muffin, and then couldn't turn down the plastic container filled with the rest of the muffins which Cecile gave her to take home.

When she realized she'd been here for almost an hour, she got ready to leave. She'd hoped to see Reed, thought he would have come to the kitchen by now. Thought that Pennington might have told him she was here. But perhaps he wasn't around.

"Is Reed here?" she asked, bracing herself for the answer.

"He's here, but he keeps himself locked away in the library, like I told you," whispered Cecile.

"Locked away?" And in the library? This didn't sound like the man she had come to know. "Maybe I should go and see him. Do you think I could disturb him?"

"Go ahead and disturb him," Cecile encouraged.

Jenna knocked on the library door, and when he didn't answer, she knocked harder again, and heard his terse, "Come in." He turned around as she walked in.

"Jenna?" He sounded happy. Looked fine, if a little disheveled as he stood up. He held out his hand, which was absurd, because they didn't ordinarily shake hands. But she took it. And he held on, slightly longer than was necessary for a normal handshake. "I thought I heard your voice," he confessed.

He'd heard she was here and he hadn't come out to see her? This took her by surprise. "I came to see Cecile," she said, her eyes raking over his appearance. He didn't look as if he was suffering. He didn't look like a wounded soldier, or too rough, or as if he hadn't slept.

"Your hair," he said slowly. "You cut off the ends."

She nodded.

"Why?"

"I have a new job," she announced, feeling pleased with herself.

"A new job? Hey, congratulations."

"Thank you."

"We have a new maid."

"So I heard." Now that she allowed herself to drink in his appearance, she realized that he looked *good*. He looked better than she last remembered, when he'd come to see her. He didn't seem to be suffering, not in the way the Cecile had described. "You look fine," she said. "Cecile…Cecile said you weren't doing so well."

He angled his head. "Cecile said that?"

"She said you were moping around."

He exhaled slowly. "I've had a lot of things to deal with."

"You did that interview with the local paper," she stated, suddenly remembering. He'd cleverly called Olivia out on her fabricated story about Jenna being the reason for the break-up. "You never do interviews."

"I hate publicity."

"I know you do, that's why I was surprised."

"I felt it was my duty to say something." He looked at her as if he had more to say, but didn't.

"Thank you," she said.

"I'm glad you came by, Jenna."

"I wanted to say goodbye to Cecile."

They fell silent for a few moments.

"I've missed you. There hasn't been a day when I haven't thought of picking up the phone and calling you."

This was so wonderful to hear. "Why haven't you?"

"I was doing what you asked me to."

"And what was that?" she asked, shakily. Memories came flooding back, of him finding her lying on the floor eavesdropping on his conversation with Olivia. Being around him was having that effect on her body again, affecting her heartbeat and her breathing.

"You said we were different," he said, talking a step towards her. "You said we were the haves and have-nots, as if that defined us."

"I know." She pressed her lips together, wanting to take a step towards him, wishing he hadn't stopped where he was, that he would come closer. She didn't feel like that anymore, that they were so different. "The way Cecile spoke about you, she had me worried. I thought you might be pining away for me." She smiled as she said it, then shrugged for the double who-cares-anyway effect.

"*Me, pining,* for you?" he asked, making her heart plummet.

She bit her lower lip, feeling foolish again, until he stepped towards her, and boldly took her hand. "I don't pine, nor am I a wounded soldier." He gently squeezed her hands, and tilted his head back slightly. "Cecile got you worried?"

"She really did."

He looked down at her. "I've missed you, but I tend to do all that feeling sad stuff on my own, without anyone knowing. Without a hint of the dramatic."

"That's how I remember you, non-dramatic."

"You thought of me, then?"

She turned her face up at him, felt herself go soft, and giddy, as her body started to respond to him. As hard as she had tried to forget this man, as much as she had intended to come here and say goodbye, she couldn't. "You're hard to forget."

"You are, too." He lifted her hand, and his lips brushed against her unsteady fingers. "Tell me to stop, if I'm overstepping my boundaries."

She stared at his lips, stared at his eyes, and remembered it all. "I brought back your bike."

"You didn't need to."

"It was on loan," she reminded him. "I don't need it anymore."

"Not even to get to the Town Hall?" he asked.

She pulled away. "How did you know I was working at the Town Hall?" She hadn't told him that.

He reached for her hands again, "Francine told me, when she recommended a few candidates for the maid's job here."

Jenna relaxed. "Oh, I see…Is Hyacinth Fitzsimmons difficult to work for?"

"I don't know, why?" he asked, his face as impassive as ever.

"I'm working for her."

He shrugged. "If anyone can put up with her, I'm sure you can." His hands slid up her arms, fueling the fire that was starting to build inside her. This felt nice. It felt nice, being here, standing so close to him, talking like this, instead of tip-toeing around on eggshells. "I should go," she said, not because she particularly wanted to, but because it seemed to be the right thing to say.

"Don't go. Spend the afternoon here," he replied, throwing the crazy idea into the air, making her consider it. Except that she hadn't come here to do this. She'd come here to say goodbye, but her legs started to wobble, and the feel of his hands on her arms made her skin tingle. It felt warm, and familiar and comforting, standing mere inches from him, almost within his arms and falling under his spell.

And then she wondered who she was kidding.

But knowing that neither his parents, nor Pennington would be here to burst through the door, gave her a touch of daring. She laughed. "Spend the afternoon with you?"

"You're here now, and you haven't told me to stop holding your hands, and you don't seem to mind me kissing your fingers. I'm starting to think you might have come here because you wanted to see me."

"I came to say goodbye."

"Do you believe that?"

She bit her lip.

"You don't believe that," he murmured, his gaze landing on her lip. "Tell me you don't believe that."

"I don't believe that," she echoed.

"I want to know what you've been up to, and what you're doing next, and about this job of yours and how you've been." He was speaking fast, as if he wanted to make the most of it now that she was here.

She could easily stay here, after all, she didn't have anything to do this afternoon, apart from some preparation for her test. She wondered why it had taken her so long to come back to him, and as they stood only a few inches apart, all she could do was focus on his lips, so tempting, and full. He had been in her thoughts each night as she laid down to sleep. "And I want to know what you've been up to."

"I was hoping you would come back to me. It wasn't easy, staying away from you, but I knew you needed your space, Jenna."

"I've missed you more than I want to admit," she told him. She yearned for his kiss. Yearned for the thing she had been dreaming of up until now. He moved his head away, fire burning in those blue irises. "Well, that's an admission if ever I heard one." His breath was hot and sweet, and she caught a hint of his aftershave, felt the blood race through her veins, felt her belly flip. "I haven't given up," she said, feeling slightly tipsy and unsure.

"On what?"

"On us, if there is going to be an *us*."

He breathed out loudly, as if she'd smacked the air out of him with her words. "There's going to be an us," he said, his hands sliding to her hips and resting there, "if you're willing to give me a chance."

While foolish courage flowed through her, she tossed another admission at him and wondered what he might make of that. "I've wondered what it might be like, to kiss you, and be kissed by you."

His eyes glittered at the invite. "Maybe I should resolve that curiosity for you?" His hands wrapped around her waist as he pressed gently against her. Her lips parted involuntarily.

"Do you want me to, Jenna?"

She couldn't speak, but moistened her lips in answer. The room disappeared, and it was just him and her, with his body pressed against her. Her insides were like a raging inferno, and he hadn't done more than put his arms around her. Everything she had been holding back about him, suddenly unleashed, and all the things about him, his face, his voice, his touch, it all magnified. She was caught up in a Reed-vortex.

Then he kissed her, his mouth covering hers as if he owned her. It wasn't a gentle playful first-time brush of lips, this was full-on, his mouth and hers, lips and tongues dancing, the taste of him, sweet as honey, warm, and soft. She leaned into him, pressing harder, wanting to soak it all in; his scent, his touch, his everything. She moaned against his mouth because it was so much more than anything she had imagined.

They pulled apart, breathless, and hungry, and speechless.

Then kissed again, and again, and again.

"I see you were busy all afternoon," said Cecile, watching him sit down to dinner. "And Jenna didn't leave until much later."

"You were timing us?"

"I was doing no such thing."

"We were talking."

"Hmmm." Cecile made a noise as if she didn't believe him. Then, "She's good for you. I like her."

"That makes a change."

"*She* is a nice change from your previous girlfriend."

"I'll take that as a compliment," he replied, diving into his dinner.

"And I'll take that as confirmation of your new girlfriend."

He paused, but only to smile. He had asked Jenna to stay and have dinner with him, but she had been adamant that she had to leave. Something to do with prepping for an online exam.

They'd spent the afternoon talking, and making out, and making plans.

"I'll leave you to have your dinner in peace," said Cecile. "I have laundry to sort out." As she walked out, she stopped by his side. "Jenna tells me she's working for Hyacinth Fitzsimmons."

"That's what she said."

"Hyacinth isn't hiring. At least, she wasn't recently. I know this because my friend's nephew was looking for work to do over the summer, and he looked for work at the Town Hall."

"Oh, really?" Reed responded, nonchalantly.

"Yes, *really*."

"Maybe your nephew might have better luck next time."

She touched his shoulder for a fleeting moment. "I smell something."

He looked up at her. "Keep it to yourself, Cecile."

She grinned. "I'm proud of you, Reed."

# EPILOGUE

## TWO MONTHS LATER...

"*M*ontana?" Jenna felt uncomfortable. They were going for a walk by the bay, after a late lunch at The Olive Tree.

"Yes. Come with me."

She swallowed and felt her heart lurch. Reed was asking her to go to Montana to meet his parents. "Your parents don't like me." And besides, why did he want her to meet his parents so soon? They'd only been dating for a few months.

"My parents don't *know* you."

"Even when they come to know me, they won't like me."

"They will love you, just like I do."

She blinked a few times, as if she had an eyelash in her eyes. *Love me* "You don't know that," she blurted out, and wondered if he'd realized what he'd said, if he'd *meant* what he said. "Because you don't know me properly yet. You don't know everything about me."

He sat her down on the wall by the bay, "I don't know everything about you?" Reed raised an eyebrow. "I know enough, Jenna, and I knew you would react like this. I might be asking a lot, but I'm not about to make an announcement, or anything, don't worry, and if you don't feel comfortable staying at the ranch, we'll check into a hotel nearby." He sat down beside her so that they faced the ocean.

"Isn't it too soon?" They spent every evening together, having dinner, and they saw one another at weekends. She had her own apartment now, and it was easier, but she never stayed over at the Knight mansion.

It was too soon, she felt, to be meeting his parents, and definitely too soon given how their first meeting had gone.

She and Reed were getting on so well. Reed wasn't just her boyfriend, he was her best friend. But still, she was wary, not wanting to take anything for granted, and wondering if she would wake up one day and discover that it had all been a dream. "Why do you want me to meet your parents?"

"I want them to know what you mean to me." The air rushed right out of her lungs.

What did she mean to him?

She was falling for him, had fallen for him, and wasn't sure when that had happened, whether it was months ago, or weeks ago. She wanted things to coast along so that she could absorb and get used to these huge changes in her life which had come about lightning fast. "You don't want to rush into anything, Reed, because of what happened before, remember?"

He shifted slightly so that he was fully facing her. "I'm not rushing, and we're not rushing into anything. You and I," he entwined his fingers in hers. "We *feel* right together. *This* feels right."

His words, like rays of sunshine, warmed every cell in her body. She placed a hand on his knee. "I love being with you, so if it will make you happy for me to meet your parents, then let's do it. Let's go to Montana."

He was pensive. "I *can* take you somewhere hot and exotic, if you want. Maybe we should get away somewhere else first, somewhere far."

"I don't need hot and exotic, and I don't need *far*. I'm happy being here. Starling Bay isn't as bad as I first thought."

"Maybe we could go next month, in June," he suggested. "The tourists are going to start arriving soon and Starling Bay will get busy. I'd rather go away then." The moment he said it, she remembered; he was supposed to be getting married in June.

She decided. "We'll go next month."

"Are you sure?"

"I'm sure."

"Thank you." He leaned forward and gave her a kiss.

"You don't have to thank me," she responded, rubbing his arm.

"You're always so understanding, and I love that about you." He got off the wall. "Kandinsky's for ice-cream?"

"The place which has sixty-four flavors of ice-cream?" Shay had mentioned the ice-cream parlor which was at one end of the bay. She'd never been because ice-cream at Kandinsky's had been a luxury. "Why not?"

"And I can show you where we're at with the old movie theater. It's a few doors down from the ice-cream parlor."

"Oooh! Can we go inside?"

"Absolutely we can."

She pushed off the wall and they set off, hand-in-hand. "I feel as if I've railroaded you into seeing my parents," he said, after a while.

"They mean a lot to you, Reed. It's fine. Besides, I've never been to Montana."

He turned and looked at her, and his lips curved up into a smile that consumed her. He meant a lot to her, it was frightening sometimes. Maybe love was like that; scary, and exciting, and filled with up-and-down moments. Sometimes she felt her heart would burst because it was so full, and other times she felt as if it would sink, because of a simple misunderstanding. Being in love was a knee-jerking, gut-wrenching roller-coaster ride.

She was in love with this man, and it was a huge turnaround in her feelings. She who had hated the boy he had once been, the one who had turned her away and humiliated her.

But she was. In love. With Reed Knight.

Life was strange like that. It had taken her full circle and now she was back at Starling Bay, except that so many things had changed, and for the better.

Thank you for reading *Maid for Him!*

I hope you enjoyed Reed and Jenna's story. If you're intrigued and want to know what happens to Rourke, don't worry! **Like his friends, he gets his own book, too.**

Rourke's book, *Love Letters*, is now available.

You can read an excerpt at the end of this book.

If you enjoyed *Maid for Him*, and if you have a moment to spare, and it's not too much trouble, please consider leaving a review. **A review can be as short as one sentence, and your opinion goes a long way in helping others decide if a book is for them.**

Thank you,
Sienna

# EXCERPT FROM LOVE LETTERS

"*I* never expected that, did you?" Rourke asked his friend Dylan, as their friend Reed walked away towards his car.

"It's not that surprising." Dylan checked his cell phone for the umpteenth time.

Rourke and his friends had just left the Blue Velvet Bar where Reed had dropped a huge bombshell; not about his engagement breaking up—he'd told them about that a few weeks ago when he'd hinted that his then fiancée, Olivia, had blamed his maid, Jenna, for the break-up. Reed had explained that his and Olivia's problems had started soon after they got engaged. But *still,* even though the break-up had been a shock, it had been nothing compared to tonight's news: that Jenna no longer worked for Reed, and, even more shocking, he had hinted of an attraction between them.

Reed had kept it vague, as was to be expected of a man like him. But the news had shocked Rourke; not so much because Jenna had been Reed's maid, but more because, up until tonight, Rourke had suspected that Jenna might have been the one sending the love notes. He'd received three now, and the third one only a few days ago. They had started on Valentine's Day with each subsequent one arriving two weeks later.

He didn't know what to make of it.

"What do you mean it's not surprising?" Rourke growled. Dylan behaved like a know-it-all most of the time, and acted as if most things didn't surprise him. Rourke didn't care what this smart aleck said this time. Reed and Jenna getting together was big news.

Dylan was still texting, and had a goofy smile on his face.

"Texting Merry again?" Rourke groaned. "I'm still here and trying to have a conversation with you." He clicked his fingers.

"Just letting her know I'll be back in half an hour."

"Why?"

Dylan looked up at him, stopped texting and put the phone away. "Because…why not? Why are you so grouchy?"

Rourke folded his arms. "Reed's news is a shock, that's all."

"It wasn't that big of a shock. I saw that coming."

"Even after the ball?"

"Especially after the ball."

"Were you and I at the same ball?" Rourke asked, because he'd seen Reed go up on stage, had seen his fiancée look stunning in that red dress, and they'd both looked like a couple in love. They'd kissed on the stage. They'd looked happy. What had he missed? "What did you see that I didn't see?"

Dylan sighed. "It was there all along. Don't you pay attention to anything?"

Rourke opened his mouth to say something, but didn't. He *did* pay attention. Mostly to women. He could scan a room within seconds of stepping into it and filter out the lookers in one glance.

"But Jenna?" he asked. That had come as a surprise. Most men had a type. He had his. His ideal woman was slim, feminine and beautiful. Of course, it could be any number of women in Starling Bay who matched that description, and it was eating him up trying to figure out who it could be that was sending the notes.

He preferred women with long hair, and a tall, slender figure. Leggy, too. He loved long, long, long legs. He'd been using his type, and interactions with the women he knew, to narrow down his list of possible senders of the love notes.

Jenna was, well…pretty, but she was also different. Her blue hair put her in the slightly crazy category. He didn't think she was Reed's type either, but maybe a man's *real* type versus the imagined type diverged in reality.

The only reason he'd considered Jenna as a possible sender had been because the love notes had started arriving soon after she had returned to Starling Bay. This was why he'd been so interested in her for the past couple of months.

And they'd gone to the same school many, many years ago. He figured it had to be someone he knew, even someone from his past. At least he hoped so. The idea of a random stalker being behind the love notes scared the heck out of him.

"What's that supposed to mean?" Dylan asked as he walked towards his pickup. Rourke followed. "She's not his type."

"Maybe she is now," said Dylan. "Or do you mean about her being a maid? Who cares about that stuff? Jenna seems like a nice person, from the little I gauged of her at the ball. I don't know her. Thing is, it doesn't matter what we think of her. Reed likes her, and we've got to be there for him."

"Yeah, of course. We do," Rourke agreed, "But he's a dark horse."

"Talking of dark horses, are you really not going to celebrate your birthday? Or do you have secret plans with a secret girlfriend?" Dylan asked.

"I don't have a girlfriend right now."

"And you're definitely not celebrating your birthday at all?"

"No, I'm not."

"Touchy."

"It's just another birthday." He didn't want a fuss; he didn't want a celebration with a big party. His parents had come over last weekend, and they'd gone to Fellini's for dinner. The popular Italian restaurant was a family favorite. Too bad his sister, Shelly, hadn't been able to make it. He'd told her it was no big deal, but she thought he was in denial, and that he was possibly going through a mid-life crisis twenty years early.

He disagreed. He was fine. Turning thirty was no big deal. No big deal at all.

"It is another birthday, you're right," Dylan agreed. "After a while, it doesn't matter and the numbers don't mean jack."

Rourke sniggered. "Of course you're going to say that because you're positively ancient, pal."

"My age doesn't bother me as much as turning thirty bothers you, *pal*. See you soon?"

"I'm always free," Rourke replied easily. "I should ask if you and Reed have time for me these days, seeing that you're both busy with your new love interests."

"You're definitely grumpy tonight. Call me when you're in a better mood." Dylan winked at him and drove away.

Maybe he was a little peeved that he could no longer claim he was in his twenties, but other than that, he was fine.

Other than this irritating little thing he now had to deal with. He walked towards his car, doubly perplexed because the mystery had suddenly deepened. He climbed into his seat and pulled the most recent notecard out of his jacket pocket.

Just like the two before it, this notecard had also been delivered to his work address. It was a pretty little card, white with colored flowers on the front. Each of the three cards had pictures of flowers, and this one also had little pink hearts.

A girlie card.

There was no printed writing inside, only a handwritten poem. This third one said:

*If I were brave, I would shine a beam,*
*And light up your path to me.*
*There's no other way to make you see,*
*That you and I were meant to be.*

The first one had been unexpected and a nice surprise. The second one had been interesting, and still a nice surprise. This third one had been a pleasant distraction from work, from turning thirty, and from his very-much-single status. It had been an uplifting boost when he'd believed that Jenna might have been a contender, when he'd thought he could pin a face to the person behind it. But now that Reed had hinted, albeit vaguely, of an attraction between him and Jenna, this line of enquiry was out of the question.

He shoved the note back into his pocket. In the general scheme of things, of life, and the new hire at work, and the properties he was working on selling, these love notes weren't important. But they were a minor irritation. Who the heck was sending them and how long was he going to put up with this situation?

With Jenna out of the equation now, it could be any number of women. He was going to have a hard time figuring out exactly who.

***Love Letters*** is available at all retailers.

# BOOKLIST

Whirlwind Kisses
Winter's Kiss
Maid for Him
Love Letters
Escape to Starling Bay (Books 1-3)
From Faking to Forever
Winter's Vow
Guarded Hearts
Table for Two
A Bouquet of Charm
Christmas Hope

For a complete list of books go to:
**http://www.siennacarr.com/books**

# ACKNOWLEDGMENTS

I would like to thank my amazing group of proofreaders who check my manuscript for errors, typos and inconsistencies.
 I am eternally grateful for their help and support:

Marcia Chamberlain
Nancy Dormanski
April Lowe
Dena Pugh
Charlotte Rebelein
Carole Tunstall

I would also like to thank Tatiana Vila of Vila Design for creating the awesome cover.

# ABOUT THE AUTHOR

Sienna Carr is the sweet romance pen name for an author who has been writing romance since 2013. She lives in the UK with her husband, three children, and a parrot.

**Connect with Me**

I love hearing from you – so please don't be shy!
You can email me at: sienna@siennacarr.com

Copyright © 2019 Sienna Carr

Maid for Him (Starling Bay, Book 2)

All rights reserved.

No part of this publication may be copied, reproduced in any format, by any means, electronic or otherwise, without prior consent from the copyright owner and publisher of this book.

The scanning, uploading and distribution of this book through the internet or any other means without the prior written consent of the author is illegal and is punishable by law.

This is a work of fiction. All characters, names, places and events are the product of the author's imagination or used fictitiously and do not bear any resemblance to any real person, alive or dead.